The Life a1
of
Carlton Russell

(Book 2)

by Barry Prokop

Contents

———Ξ———

About this book

——— ⊟ ———

This book continues the adventures of Carlton Russell. CR escapes from Fairfax, Virginia to head down to the Outer Banks, North Carolina to help his friend Roger Bennett with a little problem which soon turns into a big problem. CR has to wrestle between trying to figure out who is murdering Roger's investors while dealing with Natalie, CR's on again, off again girlfriend and her crazy antics. CR soon realizes being on vacation is sometimes more deadly than working from home. However, another murder, an irate police Lieutenant and a comely caterer, as well as the other houseguests soon turn the idyllic ocean-front house in the Outer Banks into a chaotic puzzle CR has to solve before it puts him six feet under. As you get to know Carlton, you will learn he is a man of many facets, interests, and even biases. But all in all, I think you'll find him to be an all-around good guy who is trying to make his way in the world and do good. Carlton grew up from modest beginnings. His mother was a schoolteacher and his father was a government worker. But he had ambitions. He studied hard, went to school, got laid by the time he was sixteen years old and so for all intents and purposes, a huge success. He went to college and learned some, but not really enough, knowledge to succeed in the real world. After college he started his own business and then started another business. He sold them all and started three different companies which he refers to as Earth, Wind, and Fire. You may hear about them from time to time. The places and events in the book are both real and imagined. For the most part they are real if they actually existed and imagined when they didn't. The people in the book are taken from Carlton's memory of events as they happened, and he decided early on to change their names to protect the innocent or the guilty. I will leave it up to the reader to decide which is which.

So, sit back and listen to Carlton Russell relate his adventures, thoughts, and idiosyncrasies in his own words. I hope you will love his adventures as much as he does.

Enjoy

Barry Prokop

This is dedicated to all those adventures and mysteries that don't include villas in the south of France, super spies, million-dollar heists, and yachts. This is for the rest of us that lead a fairly normal life. Well, except for Carlton Russell.

The Life and Times of Carlton Russell

(Book 2)

Chapter 1

THELMA PINKERTON TOLD me if I ever headed down to the Outer Banks I had to stop by the Morris Farm Market. She said it was the best farm market around and that in 1982, under the shade of two old pecan trees, Walton and Ginger Morris started selling sweet corn out of the back of their old Ford pick-up truck. Today they sport all different kinds of fruits, vegetables, and pies. I was tempted to stop by Powell's Farm Market since they were the first market I came to, but I trusted Thelma, so I waited until I saw the Morris Farm Market. I got there just as they opened and picked up some blueberries, strawberries, and plums. I also picked up an apple pie. I looked at the wine and they featured North Carolina wine. Now, I'm not an expert in wine but I don't remember anybody touting North Carolina as a leading wine producer. I let it go as an experience I may never have.

I continued on my journey and crossed over the Wright Brothers Memorial Bridge early Tuesday and ended up in the Outer Banks, North Carolina. For centuries, adventurers had been drawn to the Outer Banks, from the early European settlers, to the aviation-crazed Wright Brothers, to pirates. The Outer Banks is also home to one of America's oldest and most baffling mysteries, the establishment and subsequent disappearance of "The Lost Colony." The Southern Outer Banks, particularly Ocracoke Island, was notorious as the stomping grounds for some of history's most infamous pirates. Notable swashbucklers from Calico Jack to Anne Bonney and Mary Reed. I was hoping my visit would not be that noteworthy.

I went down Currituck Highway and turned left on First Street. The word Currituck means "Land of the Wild Goose." Currituck and the Outer Banks might be known for the wild horses that roam the beach, but the area actually earned its name due to its early population of wild geese when the Algonquin Indians founded it. Anyway, I followed First Street until it ended at Beach Road, or for you non-locals, Virginia Dare Trail. I took a right-hand turn and went down a couple of blocks and then turned left into one of those McMansions. It was three levels, well-maintained and painted a mellow yellow with blue trim. Only at the beach could you get away with painting the house those colors. I went in the main door and there was an elevator which I found surprising. It took a key code to get up to the third floor, and I went in to look around. I think I can optimistically say my whole townhouse would have fit on that one floor.

It was a fantastic open design with a huge bank of windows on the other side of the room that overlooked the ocean. If I wasn't mistaken, there was a collapsible wall of windows where when pushed open, the inside instantly became part of the outside. The kitchen was a centerpiece of the floor and had all top-of-the-line stainless steel appliances. The center island protruded into the room giving more working space and a feel of blending the kitchen into the living area. Off to either side there was a short hallway which I'm sure ended with bedrooms.

I dropped my suitcase with my underwhelming collection of clothes and started to explore. I first went off to the right and found two huge master suites each with their own bathroom and Jacuzzi. One bathroom had a toilet and urinal and the other one had a toilet and bidet. You can really stretch out in a place like this, apparently. It's funny the things you notice when you look through the house. That was probably one of the things I would remember most about it, or so I thought.

Next, I went back out to the main living area and pulled open the sliding glass doors. While you could hear the ocean in the background with them closed, you could really hear it up front and personal with them open. The waves crashing on the shore. The sea gulls calling in the distance. I wandered back over to the kitchen and opened the refrigerator door. It was fully stocked. Well, fully stocked for me. It had vodka, diet tonic and limes. I fixed myself a drink. I walked to the back deck and contemplated what a hell of a week I'd had. This was the perfect relaxing atmosphere I needed to recharge.

I sat in one of the Phat Tommy Recycled Poly Resin Balcony Chairs. I only knew the chair name because last week at the Blue Iguana, Heidi Poncar had educated me at length about them as well as the vacation she'd just had down here in the Outer Banks. It seems her highlight was the chair and mine was going to be the urinal. There were eight, chairs not urinals, on the balcony in different colors. Nice. I chose the one near the middle. It was turquoise. I sat there and admired the view. I could even smell the ocean and in my own imagination could feel the spray. I finished my V&T and went back in for another. I noticed his choice of vodka was Grey Goose. I tipped my hat to Roger, metaphorically, for his attention to detail. I then went to explore the remaining rooms.

A quick glance in the first bedroom told me it was just a mirror image of the ones on the other side of the house. I looked in the last bedroom and stopped short. There was a woman in a bikini laying on the bed. Normally, I'd be excited by this. My thinking would be, Roger really knew how to pay attention to detail. The ocean, Grey Goose, and a lovely shaped woman laying half naked on the bed.

The fly in the ointment was I could tell even at this distance she was dead. What tipped me off was the purple face and a brightly colored scarf tied tightly around her neck.

This was not the way I wanted to start the week.

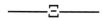

Chapter 2

I LOOKED AROUND the room and saw what appeared to be her cell phone on the dresser. It had one of those wallet cardholders on the back. I went over and gingerly picked it up and pulled the cards out until I found her driver's license. Using my cell phone, I took a picture of it and then put everything back the way I had found it. I went into the bathroom and pulled a couple of tissues out and made sure the credit cards and license were wiped clean. A picture of the dead girl might prove useful, but I realized that would be kind of macabre. There didn't seem to be any luggage or clothes I could see. I backed all the way out of the room and went back into the kitchen.

I stood there and thought a moment, then went to the refrigerator and pulled out the Grey Goose, diet tonic, and the limes. I opened the cabinet underneath the sink and found a plastic bag and dumped everything into that. I wiped down the refrigerator handles and then went out to the balcony and wiped down the chair. Not that I think it needed it, but just to be extra cautious. I closed the sliding glass doors, wiped the handles and looked around the house trying to play back in my mind what I had touched. I grabbed the bag on the counter, my suitcase, the glass with my V&T in it, and retraced my steps back down to the car, making sure any surface that had been touched was wiped clean. I looked around again for any security cameras but didn't see any. The house and area around it were eerily quiet.

I got into my car, turned around and pulled out of the driveway. I drove down the block and pulled into the Second Street beach access lot. I looked at the driver's license picture from my iPhone. Her name was Kathleen Kidd. 32 years old, five foot seven, 116 pounds, green eyes, black hair, short and cropped. Dead.

This can't possibly be happening, I thought to myself. The paranoid part of me thought I was being set up. Somehow Roger knew this woman was dead and for some strange reason wanted me to find her. Was it possible Roger killed her? Maybe a lover's quarrel. It was probably sheer dumb luck no one had seen me entering or exiting. Dammit, I wanted to enjoy the sun and the beach, not be involved in some sordid murder. What to do, what to do? To help me decide and to stall for time, I called Roger.

Before I get into that, a little explanation is probably in order as to why I'm down in the Outer Banks in the first place. For those who followed my adventures in the previous book, this is going to be old news to you. For those who are reading this for the first time, although I don't know why you would be reading this for the first time since this is Book Two and who reads Book Two without reading Book One? Maybe someone told you, you had to read about Carlton Russell and the only book you could find in the used bookstore was Book Two. But it's like grabbing a seat in the theater in the middle of the movie. It just isn't done. So, let me do it this way. If you read Book One go to the next chapter. If you didn't, hang in there and we will catch you up. But I digress.

Roger Bennett had been trying to talk to me for a while, and we had finally connected last Saturday at the Blue Iguana.

I turned in my stool and saw him across the restaurant talking to a couple. He was just saying his goodbyes and heading back over to the bar area. I motioned to a stool next to me. He grabbed his empty glass from another barstool area, sat down and ordered another Fonseca Bin 27 Port. He sat and watched Eddie pour it out and then eagerly took a sip. He closed his eyes and took a deep breath. "Now that's what I needed."

"Oh, tough day?"

"Tough week. No, let me correct that, tough month."

"What's up?"

Roger scratched his head. "I don't know. You know how you sometimes get that feeling something is wrong, but you can't really put your finger on it? I got one of those."

Roger Bennett blew in about six years ago from North Carolina. Was tall and lanky and had the typical North

Carolina drawl that sometimes almost put you to sleep. He was a self-proclaimed handyman who was in pretty high demand, and while he could do almost anything, he really liked kitchen redesigns. He wasn't married and didn't have any kids I knew of but came from a large family. While he wasn't the brightest bulb in the box, he knew his limitations. Whenever he felt out of his depth, he always consulted someone for advice. Apparently, in this situation, that person was me.

I welcomed this conversation because it would take my mind off my townhouse. "What seems to be your concern?"

"I got this property I acquired about three years ago. I couldn't really afford it, so I sold weeks to other people. Michael and Blueberry Attorneys at Law help me set it up. Craig Overdorf is the one who set me up with them to get all the documents and I's crossed and the T's dotted."

I knew what he meant but didn't want to interrupt his train of thought. "That sounds like a good deal."

"It is. Or was. I've ten different investors and they each get four weeks during the year. Like a timeshare arrangement. That income pays for most of the mortgage. I own half the house and they each own five percent. I fix up and maintain the home myself. It's a real beauty down in the Outer Banks. Since there are three floors, each with separate kitchens, two of them could be in there at any one time. I reserved the top floor for me exclusively."

"And what's the problem?"

"It may be nothing, but it appears my investors are starting to drop like flies. One got killed by a hit-and-run driver in DC and the other jumped off the tenth floor in an apartment building in New York."

"Coincidence?"

"Maybe. You see when one of the investors dies, their equity is distributed among the other investors."

"I don't think that's normally how it works, Roger. Can't you sell shares to additional investors?"

"No, the crackerjack attorneys put a clause in there that all investors would have to agree to it, and they don't."

"Roger, so if all the investors die but one, they will own half the house?"

"That's one thing I didn't anticipate. Apparently neither did the attorneys. If that happens, it's possible they could end up with the house. You see, their equity goes up, but their payments don't. It could quickly get to a point where I would have to sell them my share just to get out from underneath it."

I whistled. "What can I do to help you? I can recommend a great lawyer."

"There may be nothing wrong. It may have just been coincidence or just my paranoia. But if you can take the time to look into it, I would appreciate it."

"Let me think about it and I'll get back to you in the next couple of days."

The conversation then turned to Al Figlio, and how in the world he ever got Serena to sleep with him. She was a hottie and Al was just, well Al. We decided it had to be poor lighting and strong drinks. With that brilliant deduction, I finished my V&T and headed back to the Marriott.

———✠———

Chapter 3

I THOUGHT ABOUT Roger's offer and accepted it. That's how I happened to be in the Outer Banks. Oh, there's also going to be a lot of stuff in here about Denise, E, Natalie, and other people and events which were covered in Book One. Seriously, you need to read Book One, it's good stuff. But if this is the only game in town, I will try my best to fill in the holes for you as we go along.

So, back to Roger. Remember Roger? He was the one giving me the investor names who were going to be down there that week.

Roger picked up on the third ring. "Roger ol' buddy, old pal. I'm down in the Outer Banks," I exclaimed cheerfully.

"That's great, I'll bet you made good time. Especially driving down there off-weekend. How's the weather?"

"Sunny and in the 70s. You should come down."

"I wish I could. I'm working on a renovation that has a pretty tight deadline. The home's owner is an absolute nightmare, and if I'm not there every day to keep everybody on track, she'll take advantage of the situation and get them to start working on projects that aren't part of the contract. Then I have to go back and clean everything up after that. It's not worth it, so I am running herd over them. Believe me, I would rather be there than here but the amount of money she's willing to pay for this renovation is ridiculously high. What can I say? I'm a slave to the almighty dollar."

Okay, that made me feel better that Roger probably wasn't involved. I know, everyone always tells me I have a suspicious nature. "I was thinking before I went to the house, you should probably give me a quick list of who I should be looking out for on the other floors."

"Okay, hold on just a minute, I've got the list around here somewhere. I know I should remember everybody's name and I do, their first name. Sometimes the last names trip me up since I don't use them often. Where is that damn list? Ah, here it is. Okay, you're ready?"

I took out my notebook that was laying on the seat beside me. "Shoot."

"The first four are going to be down there starting on Wednesday, tomorrow. They are there for two weeks. Then the next four are down there from that Wednesday to the next Tuesday. So we will have a full house. We are also having an investor meeting on that Saturday. So here are the names: Isadora and Theodora Crump, Hanover Bennet (no relation),

Mr. and Mrs. Harry Patterson, Kathleen Kidd, Penny Truman, Decker Alvarez, Hastings Meadow, Love Tablue, Benny Goodman, and Olaf Raehnegin.

"You don't have to worry about Benny and Olaf because they're dead."

"Yes, you mentioned one was a hit-and-run, and the other one jumped off the building. When did this happen?"

"One happened two weeks ago and the other was about a month before that."

"Have the police found out anything?"

"No, to the best of my knowledge they are both still unsolved."

"Did they question you about it?"

"Yes, Benny was the first one that died. Apparently, he was out jogging and got run over. His brother called to tell me about it. I didn't really get any questions about his death until Olaf died. Some crackerjack detective connected the two, I think he connected them through Olaf's email and then both of the police departments contacted me to get any information I had. I wasn't able to tell them much other than the fact they were both investors in the beach house."

"Had any of the other investors been in touch with them?"

"I did ask that question, and in addition to me, almost everyone had reached out from time to time to connect with them. There wasn't anything they could find in the emails that pointed to one person or another."

"Huh, well based on that, I guess it would be logical to think of it as a coincidence."

"I know, I know. I'm just being a worrywart, but I would rather be safe than sorry."

"I hear you. Anyway, back to the matter at hand, are you sure there's enough room at the house for everybody?"

"Oh sure. There's plenty of bedrooms. There's four on each floor, and they're not all going to be there at the same time."

"Doesn't everybody mind sharing the floor with everyone else?"

"No, it's worked so far and besides, each of them gets a couple of weeks down there by themselves. During those weeks they have the whole floor. This is the only time they share it and that only happens every other year."

"Okay, I'll call you tomorrow so I can get a little bit better background on each one of these people, so be ready to give me a data dump."

"Sure, sure. Anything you need."

"Is anyone supposed to be down there today?"

"No, you have the place to yourself tonight."

"Huh, that's strange. I just drove by and there was a car in the parking lot. I thought I saw someone sneaking into the house. Well, it was probably just the cleaning crew." I lied.

Roger said in a perplexed voice, "No, they were there yesterday. I really don't like the sound of that. I think I'll just call the police and have them check it out before you go in."

"That actually sounds like a great idea, Roger. I would hate to interrupt some house crasher."

"We do get those from time to time. Some people see a house is empty, and they crash in for a free weekend. I had it happen once or twice in the past. Let me call the cops and I'll call you back when the coast is clear."

I pulled out of the Second Street beach access and pulled into an empty driveway down the street from Roger's house. This way I would be able to see when the police showed up. You probably noticed when reading down the list of his investors, Kathleen Kidd's name was on it. She was supposed to have arrived tomorrow. If that was the case, why was she showing up dead today?

About fifteen minutes later a police cruiser rolled up to the house. I waited about ten minutes after that and then pulled out of the driveway and drove up to the house. I left the booze in the trunk and took my time getting my suitcase. I had just finished rearranging the inside of the car for the fifth time when the police officer came back down. I closed the car door, locked it, and looked up in feigned surprise. "Hello, officer, is there a problem?"

"No sir, just doing a house check."

"Did you find anything interesting?"

The officer didn't answer the question. "Can I ask you sir, why you are here?"

"Sure, I'm a friend of Roger Bennett and he invited me down for the weekend."

"Could I please see some ID?"

"Certainly. Is there a problem?" I pulled out my Virginia's driver's license and handed it to him.

The officer scrutinized the license and handed it back. "Mr. Bennett called the station a little bit ago to ask us to check on his house. He wanted to ensure there hadn't been any break-ins."

"I see. Should I get Mr. Bennett on the phone to confirm he invited me?"

"No sir, that won't be necessary. If you weren't invited, you wouldn't have the keycode for the elevator to get to your floor. However, if you don't mind, I will escort you in." Now that was sneaky. He didn't want to call me a liar, but he was darn sure going to ensure I belonged there.

"No, Officer"—I looked at his name tag—"Fenton. I don't mind at all." My mind was racing. Was this a trap? Was Officer Fenton trying to get me to admit there was a body inside? He didn't seem particularly distraught or excited when he came out of the house. I tried to play it cool and grabbed my suitcase. I walked ahead of him to the house, taking care not to hurry nor be too slow. I went inside and looked around like it was the first time I had been there. I finally identified the elevator and pushed the open button.

Once inside, I punched in the keycode to get to the top floor. Officer Fenton watched me closely each step of the way. My mouth was dry as the elevator doors opened, and I walked into the main living area.

"Well, here we are safe and sound," I said cheerfully and fully expecting Officer Fenton to turn around and leave.

"Yes sir. Have you been here before?"

"No, this is my first time."

"Well, since I was just here, let me show you around really quick. The other two floors have the exact same layout. I checked them also."

Bells started ringing in my head. He pointed to the first set of bedrooms I went into. "They've got a double master over on that side."

"Oh?"

"Yes, each has its own bathroom. And you're not gonna believe this, one of them has a urinal."

Okay, it's a guy thing.

"This side, over here," he said, walking closer to the other set of bedrooms, "is the same as the other side. Here let me show you." He ushered me ahead of him into the bedroom with the dead body. I closed my eyes as I went through the door.

"Sweet, huh? And it's got a great view."

I opened one eye and then the other. All I saw was a bed against the bank of windows overlooking the ocean. The body was gone. I looked around the room, but there was no sign that anyone had been there. I tried to hold my surprise and anxiety in check. "Yes sir, that is quite a view." I stifled a yawn. "You know officer, I've had quite a long drive down here and I'd love to get a quick nap in if you don't mind."

"Oh sure, no problem."

He and I backed out of the room and went into the main living area.

"Thank you for checking on the house, Officer Fenton. I know Roger appreciates your service. So, I am the only one here, it looks like."

"Yup, unless you have a body stuffed in the closet or something." He laughed. I laughed too but mine sounded a little bit more hysterical than his.

Officer Fenton said he hoped I had a great vacation and left the way he had come in.

As soon as the elevator doors closed, I mouthed the words, 'What the hell?'. My anxiety overcame me to the point where I almost had a panic attack. I grabbed my cell phone and pulled up the picture of Kathleen Kidd's license just to make sure I hadn't dreamed anything up. I ran back into the bedroom and checked the closets. Nothing. I went through the whole floor, looking under beds, in closets and behind curtains. Nothing. I even lifted the toilet lid and looked inside. Okay, I had looked everywhere else, so I figured I might as well be thorough. The body had vanished.

I knew one thing; I wasn't staying in that place tonight. I waited about a half hour before I went downstairs and looked around to make sure Officer Fenton had left.

Roger called a short time later to tell me the coast was clear. I asked him if it would be a good idea to change the top floor keycode and he agreed. He gave me the new keycode and hung up. I got in the car and drove around, thinking. I noticed a bunch of the houses had a Sun Realty sign posted prominently in front with the phone number and a reference number. On a long shot, I called the number.

"Sun Realty, Stephen speaking. How may I help you?"

"Yes, I'm looking to rent a house for the two weeks."

"Certainly, sir, which area would you like to rent in?"

"Kill Devil Hills, between the highways."

"An excellent choice. Let me check our listings there. Which date did you have in mind?"

"Now, through the next two weeks."

"Sir, did you say now? As in today?"

"Yes, indeed I did."

"Sir, most people asking for reservations are looking a couple of weeks to a couple of months out. I'm not sure we can accommodate you."

As he was talking, I could hear the keyboard clicking in the background as he furiously typed in his filters to see if any houses were available.

"Sir, I have found a small house in Corolla. It is a lovely location right on the beach."

"No, it's got to be Kill Devil Hills."

More typing. "Sir, if I can ask you to hold a minute, let me check with my manager to see if there have been any recent cancellations."

Before I was able to utter a response, Stephen put me on hold, and I heard happy beach music. Was that Bob Marley? About two minutes passed before he came back. "Sir, my manager has informed me earlier this morning we did have a cancellation on Sir Walter Road. That is right between First and Second Street, and it is between the highways. The couple who had rented it had to leave early, so they will not be able to take advantage of the rest of their two-week rental. If you would like that cottage, we could offer you a discount. It wouldn't be for a full two weeks, but it would be for the rest of this week and all of next week, checking out on that Sunday."

"Perfect." I said. "Let's do it. "

Steven told me sheets and towels would be extra, and I said to add it in. He asked if I needed housekeeping during those two weeks and I said no. He asked if I wanted a fruit basket. Really? I declined. He tapped his keyboard a couple more times and quoted me a price. I cringed inwardly at the price. "And that is with the discount?" I said weakly.

You may wonder why I didn't just pack my bags and go back to Virginia. I didn't have any dog in this fight. No one would blame me if I just walked away. Well, that isn't exactly true. I would blame myself. There have been very few times in my life when I have backed down from a sticky situation, right or wrong. Something was wrong here, and possibly I might be able to help fix it or at least get justice for Kathleen Kidd. That did give me pause for a minute now that three people were dead and whoever was doing this didn't seem to have any reservation about knocking people off. And I certainly didn't want to be one of those people. But, right or wrong, I think I'm as clever as the next person and it just stuck in my craw that this person might possibly get away with this. So at the end of my internal debate, I realized while this series of events were not of my making, I was going to face it head on and see it through. That whole thought process took longer to write than it actually went on in my head. *She who shall not be named* used to tell me I was like a dog with a bone. I'll blame it on a genetic character flaw.

After that internal debate had been settled, I pondered a minute if I could get away with putting the cottage on my Adar Investments corporate credit card. While the thought of me giving Flavia a stroke when she saw it made me smile, I decided against it. I pulled out the Blowhard Technology corporate credit card and used that instead. Moe would probably blow a gasket as well when he saw it, but I thought I would be able to justify it under research. Wind and the Outer Banks, there had to be something I could make of that. Of course, it would mean I would actually have to do some research while I was down there.

As I am writing all of this down, I have come to the realization some readers may not know the people I am talking about, like Flavia and Moe, since they didn't read Book One. I know, back to that old argument again. But let me just say I have put a list of characters at the back with descriptions for everyone to remind themselves who is who. In short, Flavia and Moe are the CEOs of a couple of companies I work with. I actually own the companies, but they run them. I learned early on that while I was very good at creating businesses, I was terrible at managing them. That requires a completely different skill set and patience I don't have. So, I find individuals that do have that skill set, let them run the company, and get handsomely compensated for it. I try to stay out of their way is much as possible, but since I own the companies, they have to put up with me from time to time. I fly under the radar as their executive consultant. For all the employees know, the CEOs own the companies and that's fine by me.

With all of the financial arrangements out of the way, Stephen said someone would run a set of keys over to me within the hour. They would leave them under the doormat on the upper level. I cruised around Kill Devil Hills, poking in and out of different shops for the next couple of hours. I took the opportunity to cruise over to the Publix's grocery store on Croatan Highway for some provisions. I got a dozen eggs, sausage, Spam, some Bay English muffins, milk, bread, an assortment of condiments, cheese, charcoal, lighter fluid, french fries, buns, hotdogs, Bubba burgers and Blue Bell vanilla ice cream. That should be good enough for the first day or so.

If I haven't mentioned it before, I'm a breakfast kind of person. By the time I got back between the highways and found the cottage, the sun was over the yardarm—long past breakfast time but just in time for a cocktail. I took all the groceries up to the upper level, found the house keys, unlocked the door and went inside. I put away all the groceries except my Grey Goose vodka, diet tonic and limes. I looked in the freezer and the icemaker had been doing its job. I looked through the cabinets, found a glass, and fixed myself a cocktail. While sipping on it, I took the opportunity to look around and hoped the results this time would be a little bit more positive.

The cottage was a typical beach box. That's a local term that basically means it's a square set up on stilts, or pylons as they call them. The ground level, depending on how close you are to the ocean, is used just for storage. The main living area is on the upper floor. I am not going to say it was depressing, it was just different than Roger's McMansion. The whole upper floor of this cottage could fit in Roger's living area. But somehow, it seemed nice and cozy. It seemed just right for the beach. It had four bedrooms, two and a half baths, and the middle of the cottage was open and included a kitchen, eating area, and a living room.

The house was decorated with white curtains, indeterminate green/gray colored walls with beach decorations which included colorful fish and sea turtles. There was also a lot of local art that adorned the walls. The three bathrooms had bowl sinks and one was in the shape of a fish. There was a large, high definition curved-screen TV which dominated one wall, and the information on the counter indicated while they didn't have cable, all the TVs in the house were smart TVs and you could access your favorite service like Hulu, Netflix, and the Disney Channel using your own login. Each of the rooms also had Alexa Echo Dots in them, and they were connected to the heating and air-conditioning system, as well as the TV and front door lock. All the rooms sported ceiling fans and if I wasn't mistaken, the ones in the living room were made from Koa wood. It was hi-tech cute.

There were decks on both the front and the back with the back deck facing the ocean. I would guess in the promotional brochures you could say it had an ocean view but that may be stretching it just a bit. I walked out on the back deck and if I looked between two houses, I could see a patch of blue and what appeared to be the ocean. But that was about the extent of it. I noticed with amusement they also had a couple of Phat Tommy patio-height deck chairs in red and a chaise lounge. But it was certainly convenient to the ocean. I would estimate it was a short five-minute walk down Sir Walter, hang a right on First Street, cross the Beach Road and on to the beach access parking. This place even included a golf cart and beach chairs. Actually, the more I thought about it, the more I liked this better than Roger's. Roger's was nice as a grand gesture, but this was beach comfortable.

I remembered as I was driving over to the cottage I saw a restaurant called Goombays on the Beach Road which was just a short walk from the cottage. I looked again at the refrigerator and didn't see anything appealing to fix for dinner. I decided to eat out. I walked down Sir Walter Road and took a right like I was going to the beach, but on Beach Road instead of going straight across to the beach, I turned left and within a block or two I was at Goombays. They sported an outside seating area which I'm sure on nice days like this doubled as a drinking area. I walked inside and there was a reception area complete with colorful T-shirts. I turned to my right and was greeted by a hostess who asked if I wanted to go to the bar or into the restaurant. I looked to the left and the bar was pretty packed. The restaurant area off to the right was pretty full as well. As I stood there contemplating my momentous decision, a couple that had been at the bar had just paid and gotten up to leave. I told the hostess I would hit the bar. I went and sat down in one of the vacant barstools.

The bar was busy. Behind the bar, in addition to all the various bar paraphernalia, was a huge stainless-steel steamer. It appeared to be steaming pounds of shrimp at a time. It made my mouth water. The bartender came over and I ordered a vodka and tonic, extra lime. He asked if I had any preference on liquor and I told him Grey Goose. He seemed to take that in stride, nodded his head, and strolled over to his tools of the trade to prepare it. I looked around at the bar and restaurant. It was gaily decorated in beach colors with different colored chairs and tables. There were license plates from Aruba, the Bahamas, and Florida that adorned the walls. It reminded me a lot of the Blue Iguana back in Fairfax, except this had more of a beach flare.

The bartender came back with my drink and I figured out her name was Gwendolyn. I asked Gwendolyn if I could have a pound of steamed shrimp. She said certainly. The bar crowd was chatty and seemed to be mostly composed of local residents. I presumed most of the tourists were in the dining area. I admitted I came from up north and was just down for a couple of weeks to visit this tropical paradise. They nodded sympathetically feeling sorry for the fact I didn't live down here and was only visiting.

I asked if Goombays was typically this crowded on a Tuesday night and they said during tourist season it was. They lamented that the number of places where you can easily walk in from the beach to the bar were diminishing or were becoming cookie-cutter chain restaurants. The conversation turned to owners and renters in the area. The locals were not typically millionaires who bought up the beachfront property and put up big McMansions like Roger's. They much preferred the between-the-highway crowd where beach cottages were still cottages. I sipped on the V&T, which was a strong one, and lamented along with the rest of them.

The steamed spiced shrimp showed up in short order and the plate was steaming, true to its name. I dug in, peeling the shrimp, and alternated between the melted butter and cocktail sauce, which was provided. I was in heaven. The shrimp had been steamed and tossed with Old Bay seasoning. Far better than what I could do, I'll say that. Sometimes it's just not the food but the atmosphere that makes a meal great. This was one of those occasions.

I steered the conversation to different restaurants they would recommend in the area. I can pretty much guarantee I wouldn't see many of these names on the fancy brochures they were handing out at the visitor center. Although they said if I wanted to see a beautiful sunset, I needed to go to Tail of the Whale. The Goombay Smash at the end of the bar said if I wanted a great seafood meal, I needed to fix it myself. In that case, I needed to go to Billy's Seafood Market and get my seafood there. It was just a short drive over to Colington Road.

You may be wondering what a Goombays Smash is and so was I. The locals warmed to one of their favorite subjects and had Gwendolyn give me the recipe. I jotted it down on a paper napkin and then ordered one. I tried to ignore all the variations they threw at me. A Goombay Smash cocktail reminded me of a Caribbean vacation. After tasting it, I can understand why the blend of coconut and pineapple makes this a beach favorite. So, get out your own napkin or dog ear this page because here's the recipe:

1 ½ oz.	light rum
1 ½ oz.	dark rum
1 oz.	Crème de Coconut
A splash of Grenadine	
2 oz.	orange juice
2 oz.	pineapple juice

Mix all ingredients together and pour over ice. Garnish with a lime or orange wedge.

Of course, there were dissenters who said the Kill Devil Smash was far superior since it included Kill Devil Rum.

Anyway, if I wanted a great breakfast, go to Bob's or Henry's, although there was some debate on whether the Kill Devil Grill was better than both. For dinner absolutely go to Josephine's for Italian, Plaza Azteca for Mexican, Slices for pizza, and Mulligans or Steamers for seafood. That was only when you wanted a change from coming to Goombays. They all laughed at that. I asked what was good on the menu and expected to hear the typical, 'Oh everything's good,' but I was surprised at how passionate everybody was about their favorite.

The Corona said I couldn't miss if I got the Goombays Tuna Oscar. Its local tuna steak filet served over mashers and topped with lump crab meat, grilled asparagus and lemon beurre blanc. The Gin and Tonic said he had it all wrong. It's the Carbonate Shrimp that was the star of the show. She said it was Dominican inspired jumbo shrimp in garlic cream with a hot loaf of bread for dipping and vegetables. She said don't get the vegetables, get rice with it and I wouldn't regret it. The Goombay Smash didn't want to commit on a favorite. The Mimosa said to stick with the Fish and Chips, especially when they had mahi-mahi in. Gwendolyn piped in the Seafood Kingston was a popular dish as well. She said they made it with the freshest fish or shellfish sautéed with Jamaican jerk spice, coconut cream, bananas, and deglazed with dark rum. A couple of them had to refer to the menus to get the ingredients right since they had been there a couple of hours drinking, but I got the gist of it. I left Goombays with a bunch of new friends and a promise to come back soon.

I got back to the cottage and made sure everything was locked up. I fixed myself my last V&T of the evening. I went out onto the back deck and sat in the Phat Tommy and listened to the waves crashing on the distant shore. The stars were out twinkling above me and there was a light breeze out of the east. I thought to myself, this was the way life was supposed to be lived. But then my thoughts drifted over to poor Kathleen Kidd. I wondered what she had done to deserve what she got. Probably nothing. She was just a victim of circumstances and in the wrong place at the wrong time, and that's what made it more tragic. The senselessness of it all. I ended the evening on that melancholy note and went to bed.

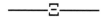

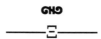

Chapter 4

THE FOLLOWING MORNING was a perfect beach day. Alexa told me the local forecast called for mid-70s with a ten to twenty mile an hour breeze out of the east. The breeze would keep the flies at bay, and the sun while warm, was not going to be hot and stifling. I noted low tide was going to be at two p.m. that afternoon. I wandered down to the beach to catch the sunrise and made a note to get out that morning and buy some beach attire to include a tie-dye shirt, swimming trunks, and flip-flops. The good news was I'd brought down sunglasses and the ball cap. Based on looking at everybody around me, I fit right in. Well, except for the dress slacks, tennis shoes, and button-down shirt.

I fixed myself a breakfast of two eggs over easy, sausage links, and toast. I found some strawberry jam left over from a previous renter and a can of Diet Coke in the refrigerator. The jam didn't have any mold or anything on it, so I guess it was okay. They had an old cast-iron skillet there, so I cooked everything on that. I love cast-iron. You only need to buy one in your lifetime and if you baby it and take care of it, it'll take care of you. I broke one of the eggs as I was turning it but quickly transferred it to my plate. The toast popped up, but I'd forgotten to buy butter, so I just had to settle with the strawberry jam. I almost forgot to add a small bowl of the blueberries and strawberry I had gotten from the Morris Farm Market. I brought everything over to the balcony-style breakfast table, sat, and had a nice leisurely peaceful meal. I thought about how I would approach this week as I was having breakfast. I figured I would spend the days over at Roger's and sneak out in the evening and stay over here. I had a feeling I would be stirring up a hornets' nest, and I didn't want to be stung while I slept. I tuned into the local radio station 102.5, The Shark, to see if there was any news about a death being discovered and there wasn't. That worried me a little bit. Unless the body was moved off the Outer Banks and stuck in a freezer, it should show up soon.

I was right in the middle of washing dishes when my phone rang.

"Where are you?"

"In the kitchen."

"What kitchen? She giggled. You don't have a kitchen, remember. Your townhouse spontaneously combusted."

I don't know that Natalie had ever particularly owned up to the fact she blew up my townhouse, but I could tell from the giggle it was her. Well, technically it was a dog named

Trouble that ultimately ended up leaving me homeless. Natalie just happened to be the catalyst which caused it to occur. Natalie, as you remember, is my sometimes girlfriend who just happens to naturally get in a lot of trouble. Many times, I am unintentionally the target of her mishaps.

Natalie continued, "I just called over at the Marriott and they said you checked out yesterday."

"I'm down in the Outer Banks, working."

As you will find out about me, working is a flexible term which can be applied to a number of different activities, paid and unpaid. In this case, I did have to do a little work for Blowhard Technologies, but my guess was the majority of my time was going to be spent unraveling what was going on over at Roger's McMansion.

"Awesome, just get me the address and I'll be down."

"But I didn't invite you."

"All work and no play make CR a dull boy," she quoted in a musical tone.

"I may be working most of the time, so you won't see much of me," I hedged. It was a good delaying tactic while I thought it through. Did I really want crazy Natalie down here in the middle of this? Granted, Natalie's body was made for the beach. Her shapely figure and skimpy bikinis were the talk of many pool parties back in Virginia. "Are you sure you can get away? Don't you have to work?" I questioned. Yeah, it was the skimpy bikini that got me. I could put her up at the cottage. Although I'm not sure how I was going to manage or explain what I was doing down there. Well, I'd think of something. I always did.

"Sure, I can. I have a couple of weeks leave." Natalie chimed in.

"You do?" I sounded surprised because I was surprised. Natalie always seemed to be taking off for this and that. A week in Florida with her girlfriends, down at Mardi Gras, skiing in Aspen, and even a concert with Tibetan throat singers in some God-awful place. I didn't think she made a lot of money in her day job.

She has her own blog and it is called Natalie's Tricks and Treats. It includes videos of her evaluating products and doing hacks to improve your house and home. I actually have never been on the blog to see it but to hear her talk, it was going to be the next Amazon. I guess with a job like that, you can pretty much set your own hours. I take that back; I did see one write-up where she was evaluating some sex toy called the grasshopper. I think I remember her using words like icky and creepy in the evaluation. It was a fairly G-rated review, but the imagery she used was memorable. I was dwelling on this when Natalie continued.

"Sure, gobs of it. There are couple of products I'm testing now which would be perfect for the beach. It will be great to get out of the studio and test them live."

"Is there anything inside the products that is liquid, fragile, perishable, and potentially hazardous, such as a lithium battery or perfume?" I asked quoting the postmaster hazmat question everybody gets asked when going to the post office to mail a package, and especially to Natalie if she was bringing foreign objects over.

"No, nothing like that." She laughed. "At least, I don't think so."

I should've known from that answer the black cloud of doom was going to follow me down from Virginia. But I ignored the sign. Don't I always? "Okay, when can I expect to see you?"

"Give me a day or two to pack and then I'll be down. Text me the address."

"A day or two to pack? Don't you already have everything you need?"

"I certainly can't wear those old bikinis and beach clothes."

I could just see her rolling her eyes through the phone. I started to say, you do know no one down here knows you or has seen your swimwear collection, but I knew it was a losing argument before I started it. "Okay, see you then." I hung up the phone half anticipating and half dreading her visit. If experience was any teacher, it wasn't going to be a dull week.

I went over to the Publix grocery store and picked up a couple of items I had missed getting the night before. I then trolled through a number of different thrift shops and secondhand stores like Mission Thrift to pick up my beach attire. I know what you're saying, I should have gone to a beach shop to get my clothes, but it just doesn't have the same look and feel as well-worn clothes. I did pick up the flip-flops though at Super Wings. When I first went by there, I was thinking it was literally a chicken wing food joint.

It took me a minute to realize everything down here has an aviation name or theme due to the fact the Wright Brothers invented and built the first ever powered airplane just down the road. The airplane was heavier than air meaning it needed a motor to get it off the ground. The Wright brothers' first flight occurred on a beach just south of Kitty Hawk on December 17, 1903. Things like aviation, first flight, wings, and Wright brothers are incorporated into a lot of the businesses down here. The cottage I rented was just a mile from the Wright Brothers Memorial. It appeared to be a strong attraction since every time I drove by, I could see cars coming and going.

As I was heading back to the cottage, Roger called. I told him I'd call him back in a few. I got to the cottage and unpacked my groceries and took the tags off of any clothes that I got. No need to advertise I got my beach shirts for two dollars apiece. I called Roger back.

"Hey Roger, what's up?"

"I know you said yesterday you wanted to get information on those that are going to be down there this weekend. It will be Isadora and Theodora Crump, Hanover Bennet, and Mr. and Mrs. Harry Patterson."

"Wasn't there another person?" Knowing full well the name he neglected to mention was Kathleen Kidd.

"Yes, Kathleen Kidd, but I talked to her this morning and she said she couldn't make it."

"Really, that's interesting." That was pretty damn interesting because I didn't know dead people could talk.

"It's not unusual for them to change their plans at the last minute."

"So, you talked to her? Did she give any specific reason?"

"Well, I didn't actually 'talk' talk to her, but she sent me a text."

"From her phone?"

"Of course, from her phone. Whose phone would she send a text from? Say, why all these questions about Kathleen Kidd? Do you know her or something?"

"I've never talked to Kathleen Kidd in my life," I said truthfully. "What time is everyone supposed to be down here?" I asked, deflecting his attention.

"They normally come down around lunchtime. When I'm down there, we have cocktails up on my floor in the evening."

"Could you arrange for them to have cocktails with me up there this evening?"

"Sure, but how am I going to explain you? I mean, I told them you were coming down but kind of left the reason open."

"How were you planning to explain me?"

"I guess I haven't really thought that part through. Maybe I can say you're my accountant or something. I really was just going to leave it up to you."

"Let's keep it simple. Tell them I am working with you to do a property value assessment."

"Hey, that's great, how did you think of that?"

"I saw it on a TV show once."

Roger chuckled. "I will text everyone to let them know and set it up for 7 o'clock."

"How will they get up to my floor?"

"Well everybody knows that code."

"I thought you just changed it yesterday."

"I did and then I texted it to everybody."

I smacked my forehead with the palm of my hand. "Roger, I need that floor to be secure. So after tonight, change and text me the new keycode but don't text it to anybody else. Got it?"

"Sure, that sounds easy enough."

I thought to myself, geez Roger, if I'm not careful you're going to get me killed down here. What I said out loud was, "Great, now give me a lowdown on these characters."

Roger thought for a moment, collecting his thoughts.

"Isadora and Theodora Crump are two sisters and are retired schoolteachers. I think elementary school, but it could be special education. I call them the CrumpITs." He laughed. "Where one goes, so does the other. They are fairly prim and proper and don't drink a lot. I get the impression they don't get out much back home and this is what they would consider a wild week for them.

"Hanover Bennet is an ex-Air Traffic Controller. He has a plane stashed away somewhere and flies down for his weeks here. I think he lives in New York. When he is here, he doesn't have a car and just Ubers everywhere. Nice guy but a little controlling, pun intended. Depending on his mood, he is either a pain in my neck or a fun guy to party with. One or two times he's brought someone down with him, but usually he comes down by himself. He's divorced and has two grown kids that work somewhere in the airline industry. He doesn't talk about them too much.

"Mr. and Mrs. Harry Patterson come down from Portsmouth Virginia every year like clockwork. Darlene and Harry are their names. She used to work for AT&T, and he's an Allstate insurance agent. In fact, he's got the insurance policy on this place. Now he's a piece of work. If you're not careful, he'll talk you into a new set of insurance policies on a house you don't even own yet but will after he gets through." He chuckled. "Darlene is his counterweight and keeps him somewhat in check. If I had to guess, she's only successful about a third of the time. When he and Hanover get into a debate, I'm never sure if it is going to end in a fight or a rendition of '99 Bottles of Beer on the Wall'. Sometimes, I think Harry just does it to bait Hanover into an argument. But I will say this about Harry, he doesn't play favorites. I have seen him make the CrumpITs blush, and Kathleen once slapped him. Harry later apologized and said he probably deserved it."

"And Kathleen Kidd?" I prompted.

I could picture Roger leaning back in his chair to contemplate that one. "Kathleen comes down every year. When she can't come down, she sends her twin sister. Those two are like night and day. I think her name is Katie or Caitlin. Kathleen is a lot more down to earth and if I was more your age, I'd probably hit on her. I think she's an actress or works in the theater. There's something musical and ethereal about her. I think it's the way she looks at you. It is like she's just looking through you. But she's fun to be around. And then there's Katie or Caitlin. Always walks around like there's a cloud over her head. She seems to have a built-in sneer and can take anything you say as an insult. Whenever she is down, things got a little tense. Anyway, we don't have to worry about that this week. Does that about cover it?"

"I guess so. You will let everybody know we will be having cocktails up on the top floor?"

"Sure, sure, I'll set everything up. I do it all the time so by now, it's pretty automatic."

I hung up the phone from Roger and thought about these characters. They seemed pretty normal. I read through my notebook at the remaining names on the list: Penny Truman, Decker Alvarez, Hastings Meadow, and Love Tablue. I sighed. I wasn't really going to get anywhere until I'd talked to these people and seen what developed.

I spent the rest of the afternoon at the beach. I walked out of the cottage and turned right. I went down one block to First Street and turned right again. I took another couple of hundred steps straight ahead and I was on the beach. Sweet. I got there right at 1:30 which was about a half hour before low tide and placed my chair about twenty feet from where the tide rolled in. At the cottage, I had found a small cooler and a couple of YETI tumblers and filled them with some V&T. I'd packed them in the cooler with ice and threw in an orange that had seen better days. The beach towel had the Little Mermaid stamped on it and was far classier than some of the other beach towels I saw. I lounged on the beach chair for a while and then took a dip in the ocean. The water was cold at first. I looked around to see lots of people frolicking in the waves, so they were either too numb to feel it or the cold wore off. I walked further out until I got to the point of no return where I either had to dive under a wave or get severely assaulted by one. I chose to dive. I came up with my teeth chattering, but it felt great. I battled the waves for another 15 or 20 minutes and then went back to my chair to warm up and let the sun do its magic.

I sipped on my V&T, peeled and ate the orange, and sipped on my second V&T, in that order. I think I drifted off to sleep because the next thing I knew there were waves crashing around my chair. I lunged to save the cooler from floating out to sea. I looked around and the tide had come back in. Funny how that works. I could see the amused looks from my fellow bathers as I dragged my cooler, sodden towel and chair back from the waves and on to higher ground. I debated setting up again but then decided I'd had enough sun for one day. I rinsed everything off at the outdoor shower at the top of the dune right after you get off the beach and onto the access road. I wrung out the towel so it wouldn't feel like I was dragging ten pounds of weight back to the cottage.

Later, back at the cottage, I laid out the towel and my swimming trunks on the back-deck railing to dry out. I looked at the time and it was around 4:30 p.m. It was too late for lunch and too early for dinner, so I fixed myself a quick PB&J and washed it down with a Fresca. I turned on the TV and tuned it in to the local news. Still no body. I was about to switch it off when they changed to national news of interest, and I'll be damned but there was Denise O'Hara sitting there talking to the host of some talk show. She was wearing a flowery dress which really complemented her blue eyes and red hair.

I had met Denise a couple of weeks earlier while in Fairfax. She invited me, sight unseen practically, to a weekend house party. One thing led to another, and after I had made her a millionaire, she decided she liked me. Don't get me wrong, it wasn't because I made her a millionaire that she liked me. Part of it was the fact I didn't take advantage of the situation. However, events overcame our budding relationship and before we could explore it any further, she was going to have to deal with a bunch of family drama and media attention. That was one reason I decided to slip away to the Outer Banks, because there was no way I was going to get in the middle of all that. Let's just say the family would not have welcomed me with open arms, and the more I faded into the background the better it would be for Denise.

The host was asking her about what she was going to do now that she was a millionaire.

"Well, I really don't consider myself a millionaire. Finding the coins is going to allow me to be able to fix up Wolf's Head Books and maybe even do something off of my bucket list." She smiled.

The host, Devon something-or-other, followed up with another question. "So, tell us again exactly how you found the coins."

Denise blushed. "My ex-husband, Ben O'Hara, had hidden the coins and when he died…" She paused and swallowed hesitantly. "He left in his will anyone that found the coins could have them. I guess I was just lucky."

"I understand the rest of the family is not very happy with your 'luck'." Devon used air quotes. "Is that true?"

"I think there is going to be a period of adjustment for us all. I certainly wish them all well, but I think everything ended the way it was supposed to."

"Some people are saying you had an accomplice who made sure the other family members wouldn't be able to find the coins. And that they were tricked and misled. What do you say to that?"

Oh no, I said to myself. Please don't drag my name into this, Denise. The last thing I need is that kind of publicity.

Denise's eyes narrowed slightly, and her voice hardened. "I think it is a horrible accusation. I think the people who said that should be —"

The host cut in, "Well folks, that's all the time we have for today. Thank you for joining us, and we look forward to seeing you in our next segment of What's Up, Washington."

I clicked the TV off, sat there and thought a minute. When I helped Denise, I didn't really think about the unintended consequences of helping her find the coins. She was basically going to be an outcast in her own family. But I think she was quickly coming to terms with that. They were going to need her a lot more then she was going to need them. I made a mental note to call her in the morning.

It was getting on toward cocktail hour, so I showered and changed. I put on my best newly bought used Hawaiian shirt, khaki shorts and some Docksiders. The Docksiders were a little tight, but I figured I could stretch them out a little with some use. I grabbed my sunglasses and drove over to Roger's house. I probably could have walked but I didn't want to give away the fact I had another place to stay. I packed some clothes in an overnight bag and took it with me. At least I could keep some semblance of the illusion I was staying there.

The driveway had four cars and a van in it, so I figured everyone must be there by now. I went in and punched in the code for the top floor. When the elevator door opened, I stood there blinking. The floor had turned into what looked like a five-star restaurant. White tablecloths, candles, and buffet trays were set out on the table. The kitchen island had been transformed into a bar and there was a full complement of wine, beer, and liquor. The Grey Goose vodka had been replenished and he even had some diet tonic on hand. Bravo Roger. I hoped no one asked where the other bottle had gone.

I stood looking around, and from one of the bedrooms emerged a woman with a white jacket on, officially looking around the room in critical appraisal until her eyes settled on me.

"May I help you?"

"Yes," I said in my most cheerful voice. "I believe I am the host for this little soirée tonight."

"Oh, you must be Carlton Russell." She smiled.

"I must be, and I am."

"Roger told me about you."

"Oh, he did? And what did Roger tell you about me?"

"Roger told me to not believe a word you said. Also, that you were the consummate flirt and would try to sweep me off my feet."

"Yeah, I get that a lot," I said dryly. "I think my reputation has been exaggerated over time."

She laughed and extended her hand. "By the way, my name is Rhonda Quick."

I shook her hand. It was soft and warm, but she had a firm handshake. "I'm glad to meet you. Are you the one responsible for this shindig?"

"I thought you said it was a soirée?" she asked as her eyes twinkled.

"Okay, soirée it is." I laughed.

"Yes, I own a local catering company and Roger has used our services the last couple of years. Each year he seems to add a little bit more to it, so each cocktail hour gets a little bit more elaborate and grandiose. I love it because it allows me to try different things. For example" —she walked over to the buffet table and lifted one of the lids—" here we have some asiago crusted jumbo shrimp and right next door we have some crab cakes. In this one we have some mussels. And with that, I have some bowls to put the mussels in as well as a really yummy butter garlic sauce to drench them in."

As she was going through this litany of dishes, I was starting to get hungry all over again. All of a sudden, that PB&J didn't look so good after all. "Wow, this puts a whole new meaning to the words cocktail hour. If nobody shows up soon, I'll be all yours."

She laughed. "Oh, they will show up, don't you worry. Based on the past, this crowd is a bunch of real chow hounds."

"Is it just going to be the other guests here?"

"Mostly, but I think Roger also invited a couple of locals. It gives it a little bit more of an authentic flair when the people visiting can hobnob with the locals and get some of the local gossip and news."

"Does that mean you will be staying throughout the whole event?"

"Oh yes," she sighed, "and I'll also be here to help clean up."

"So, you have entertained these people before? Can you give me a little insight into them?"

"Well...," she said, "I don't really want to tell tales out of school, but they're basically a nice crowd. The Crump sisters eat salad mostly. So, I prepared some mini salad bowls over there." She pointed to a table set up near the windows overlooking the ocean. "They don't drink and pretty much keep to themselves. If you want to have a conversation with them, you have to go over to them because they're not going to come to you. They are not what I would call minglers. That is certainly not the case though for Mr. Bennett and the Pattersons. They are, to put it mildly, entertaining. They both enjoy great conversations and Ms. Kidd tends to float between the different groups talking. Unless of course if her sister comes instead," she said quickly. "If so, her sister tends to sit in the corner and brood."

While this exchange was going on, two more caterers came out of a bedroom, and one manned the bar while the other hovered around the buffet. The one hovering around the buffet was counting the forks and knives and would probably count them at the end of the evening to make sure none were missing.

My eyes wandered from Rhonda over to the caterers. "You said some locals were going to be here? Do you know who they are?"

"One is Noella Weathers, who writes for OBXToday.Com and the other is the Kill Devil Hills' Assistant Town Manager, Buddy Yardley. And of course, I will be here as well to answer any questions they may have."

I smiled. "Sounds like fun." Just as I said that, I could hear the elevator doors opening behind me.

Rhonda smiled, and as she brushed past me, I heard her quietly say, "Then let the fun begin!"

While Rhonda was greeting the guests, I took the overnight bag and threw it on the bed in one of the spare bedrooms. When I came back out, more people had arrived.

Two of them I knew immediately even though I'd never seen them before. I had two people describe the guests who were staying there this weekend, but neither one of them bothered to mention Isadora and Theodora were twins and they dressed exactly alike. I looked at them closely to figure out how I could tell the difference between the two of them but failed. They were carbon copies of each other, even down to their jewelry and haircut. They were both about five and a half feet tall, slenderly built, but not frail, and looked to be about 70ish. They were both dressed in maxi-length chic sun dresses that featured a ruffled empire waist and a fun, beach-ready print to include seashells and starfish. They each wore straw sun hats with a 4-inch brim that partly covered their eyes when they looked down. They also sported Le Pliage sunglasses and a leather pair of Tory Burch flip-flops. The outfit was complete with seashell necklaces. I looked closely at the necklaces hoping to see a difference between the two, but they were a perfect matched pair. Weird. Rhonda saw me approaching and introduced me to them.

"Isadora and Theodora, this is Mr. Carlton Russell, your host for this evening."

"Yes indeed," said CrumpIt-1. "It is a pleasure…"

"…to meet you," completed CrumpIt-2. "We certainly have been a little…"

"…curious about you," completed CrumpIt-1.

It was a little like a ping-pong match, bouncing from one to the other. "Thank you. I'm very appreciative Roger allowed me to come down."

"Roger was very complementary about you, although he was a little vague…" said CrumpIt-1.

"…about what you're doing down here," completed CrumpIt-2.

CrumpIt-1 nodded.

Before I had a chance to answer or even ask them which was which, Rhonda introduced me to the other individuals. They included Buddy Yardley and Hanover Bennett. Buddy looked to be about six-foot-three, 250 pounds, broad shouldered, and in his mid-50s. He had to have played football in his youth. He wore khaki shorts and a Kill Devil Hills T-shirt. Hanover was a little bit more formally dressed in a blue and white open neck buttoned down shirt, dark blue slacks, and loafers. He was about my height and weight. He had brown wavy hair, which contrasted with Buddy's bald dome. Where Buddy had a quick smile and open demeanor, Hanover was almost the opposite, where he appeared to be very guarded and intense.

Buddy shook my hand vigorously and said, "We're certainly happy to have you down here in our lovely little town. Always a pleasure to meet a friend of Roger's."

I responded, "Yes Mr. Yardley, I actually—"

He cut me off. "Call me Buddy, everybody calls me Buddy."

"Okay, Buddy," I said hesitantly. "I just got here last night but it seems like a pretty friendly place."

"You betcha. You certainly picked the best town to visit. We got low crime, great restaurants, pristine beaches, and the tourists just love it. Glad to have them in the summer and sorry to see them go in the fall. We are a whole lot more fun to be with than that Duck crowd." With that he gave me a wink.

"I love flying into the First Flight Airport," chimed in Hanover. "It's so quaint."

I turned my eyes to Hanover. "Yes, I've seen the planes flying in low overhead. It seems to be a popular airport for the single engine planes. Looks like we are going to be sharing the house together for the next couple of days."

"Yup, I know who you are. I Googled you on the way down here but didn't find much about you. You're some kind of consultant or something, I think. So how do you know Roger, and why are you down here?"

One thing about Hanover, he gets to the point quickly. I answered vaguely, "Oh, Roger and I go back a way and we've done some business together. He thought it would be good for me to come down and check out the place."

"Really?" Hanover looked surprised. "He's never had anybody down here before to 'check out' the place before. I wonder why he's doing that now?"

Luckily at that time more people arrived. While I wasn't introduced right away, I could tell Harry and Darlene Patterson had arrived. As soon as he stepped off the elevator, he was greeting and shaking hands with everybody. It was like they were long-lost relatives. Darlene was dressed in mauve Capri pants, an intricate honeycomb dot lace transparent beach cover-up, and underneath was what looked like a mauve bathing suit top. Darlene looked to be a little taller than Harry, and they both appeared to be in their mid-60s. Harry was dressed in an interesting Hawaiian T-shirt which sported half-naked hula dancers printed on it and Tommy Bahama khaki shorts. He spied me as the only person he didn't know and apparently saved me for last. He, with Darlene in tow, caught me as I was edging my way over to the bar.

"Well, you must be Mr. Carlton Russell," exclaimed Harry heartily.

That was the second time I had gotten that question today, so I was prepared with the answer.

"I must be, and I am," I quoted.

"Well how do you do? I'm Harry Patterson, and this is my wife, Darlene."

We shook hands all around.

"So, what do you think of the place?" asked Harry.

That took me a little off guard. "The place?"

"You know, this pile. This McMansion. This house. What do you think? I wouldn't mind having a place like this to myself. Kind of a sweet location."

"Yes, it certainly is that." I was about to add to that when Harry jumped in.

"You know, talking is pretty thirsty business. We better grab ourselves a drink." Harry started walking over to the bar as Darlene and I followed.

"Yes, they have a pretty stocked bar here," I said playing the host. "If you're looking for some red wine, they have—"

Harry cut me off. "No, we're a white wine family. Besides, red wine gives me gas."

"Okay," I said hurriedly. "They have Kendall Jackson, Sterling, and I think I even saw some Fess Parker."

"Nope, none of that stuff. I'm a Woodbridge man myself. I usually get a couple of cases of the big bottles from Costco every other week and store them in the garage. Roger always makes sure there is a limited supply of my wine here, not that we would run out of it downstairs or anything." He laughed. "I brought a case or two just in case. Ah, there it is in the back, right next to that 99 Crimes, which is no slouch either by the way."

Harry grabbed the bottle and started to pour himself and Darlene each a generous portion. Then he plucked another wine glass to fill it up when I stopped him. "Thanks, but I think I am going to have a V&T."

Harry looked at me suspiciously. "Oh, so you're a hard liquor man, are you?"

"Well, I wouldn't actually characterize myself as that. I do enjoy wine every once in a while, as well."

"Well then, tonight is the night." He poured another generous portion of Woodbridge and held it out to me before I could say another word.

"Harry," Darlene said, "let Mr. Russell have his vodka and tonic."

"Nonsense. Once he takes the first sip, he won't regret it."

The wine stood suspended in midair for a couple more seconds before I took the glass.

"You down here with your wife and kids?" asked Harry casually as he looked around.

"Nope, just me."

"Really, I got a daughter about your age, maybe you could hook up with her. She is between relationships. She's a little feisty, but easy on the eyes," he said conspiratorially and gave me a quick nudge with his elbow.

"Harry!" Darlene said, horrified. "I think you need to change the conversation, now."

"Oh Darlene, I was just trying to—"

"Now, Harry!" Darlene gave Harry a look. I have been around enough married couples to know that look.

Harry sighed. I had to smother a smile. Harry changed the subject.

"So, you thinking of moving down here?"

"No, just visiting."

"Well, if you're looking to move down here, now is the time to buy."

"Harry," interjected Darlene. "Leave the man alone."

"Well I'm just saying, if you are going to buy a house down here, now's the time to buy. Of course, if you do, you're gonna need some insurance. Ask anybody around here, I'm the best. I can probably also save you money on your car insurance. What kind of car do you drive?"

"I drive a Toyota Camry."

"Aren't those new model Camry's nice? They have back up cameras, driver assist, and heated seats. Those are really nice down here when the weather turns cold. Nobody wants to drive around with cold buns, am I right?"

I said proudly, "no, mine is a 1990, so it doesn't have any of those features, although it does have automatic windows."

Harry looked at me skeptically. "Well, I guess we can put some collision coverage on it. You really need to look into getting a newer car. I know a guy."

"Harry, you don't even know why the man is down here. It probably isn't to buy a house or a new car," said Darlene in an exasperated tone.

"Sure, I do. I know exactly why he is down here," exclaimed Harry.

Now that piqued my interest. "Really, why am I down here?" I said in an amused tone.

"Well, Roger said you were down here to check us out."

Darlene gasped. "That's not what he said."

"Oh Darlene, you have to learn to read between the lines."

"He said Mr. Russell was down here as his guest," pointed out Darlene.

"Oh, you can't pull the wool over my eyes like that, Darlene. Roger is down two investors and he's on the hook for all those extra mortgage payments. Only makes sense someone would come down here investigating to see what is what. Am I right, Mr. Russell?"

I got the impression he was shooting in the dark and seeing if he would hit anything. "I think you're jumping the gun a little bit, here. Roger did ask me down to take a look at the place and possibly give him some options, but that was as far as it went. I'm not down here investigating anybody." Okay, I lied. I was down here precisely to investigate everybody. But I couldn't tell him that.

"Hmm," said Harry meditatively. "That may be the truth, but then again…"

I took a sip of my wine. I have had really good wines and really bad ones and Woodbridge was somewhere in the middle. I really could have used my V&T at that moment. Harry was just about to start on another tack of his inquisition when the elevator door dinged and opened.

I was watching Harry as he looked over at the elevator, and a surprised look overcame his features as a woman emerged. Harry said in a perplexed tone, "I thought she couldn't come."

———Ξ———

Chapter 5

I TURNED AND LOOKED at the woman who appeared from the elevator. She was short and slim with golden brown hair. She was wearing short cutoff jeans and a gray tank top with *Boat Hair Don't Care* written in white lettering across the front. She was carrying her flip-flops and had on a straw hat with a broad leather band around it. Her purse was slung over her shoulder, and the purse bag was covered with white seashells. Her oversized sunglasses were hanging from the top of her tank top. The wine glass I was holding slipped through my fingers and fell crashing to the floor, shattering into 1,000 pieces. The sound stopped all conversation as everyone turned to look at me. One of the caterers rushed over with a towel to clean up the mess. But I just stood transfixed staring at the woman.

Harry was looking at me quizzically. "You don't know her, do you?"

"Ah, no," I said automatically. "I've never spoken to her before in my life."

"Well, that's Kathleen Kidd."

I said to myself, yes that looks like Kathleen Kidd. Her hair was a little different, it was longer and lighter. But other than that, it was definitely her. I was tempted to pull out my cell phone and compare the driver's license picture to the real person but didn't have the nerve. I cursed myself because I never bothered to take a look at when the driver's license was issued. If enough time had passed, her hair could naturally be different. But the name on the driver's license was definitely Kathleen Kidd. What was I missing here?

The caterer had finished mopping up the mess and cleaning up the glass. Rhonda came over to make sure everything was all right. Darlene had wandered off and was talking to who I assumed was Noella Weathers. I just continued to stand there like a statue and stare at Kathleen.

Harry, sensing my hesitation and not wanting to miss any action said, "Say, let's get you two acquainted." Harry pulled me over to where Kathleen was chatting with Buddy. "I hate to break up the stimulating conversation which I'm sure you all are having, but I did want to introduce Kathleen to her host. Kathleen, this is Carlton Russell."

Kathleen looked coolly at Harry. "Oh, hello Harry. I'm glad to see your wife is still tolerating you."

"I thought you were a no-show this weekend and we may have to put up with your delightful sister," he said, sweetly ignoring her barb.

"Actually, we were both going to be down this weekend, but then our plans changed. Unfortunately, those plans were also canceled at the last minute, so here we are." She turned to me. "Roger mentioned you were coming down. I'm sure we'll have plenty to talk to you about." She smiled. It was a half amusing and half seductive kind of smile. It's hard to describe, but it made me feel warm all over.

I was still too dumbfounded to speak articulately, but I did catch the fact both she and her sister were supposed be down here this weekend. I needed time to think. The savior came when I realized I no longer had a drink and neither did Kathleen.

"Ms. Kidd—" I said.

"Please, call me Kathleen."

"Kathleen, can I get you a drink?"

"I thought you would never ask. I'll have a mimosa," she said gratefully, giving Harry a sharp look to let him know that that was how a gentleman was supposed to act. I could tell the glare was lost on Harry.

I went over to the bar and ordered myself a V&T, double, tall, extra lime and Kathleen a mimosa. I took a big gulp of mine before I headed back. On the way back across the room I was asking myself how this was possible. Was this her or her sister? The only thing I was fairly certain of was one of them was dead. And that's just not something you bring up in the middle of a cocktail party. Excuse me Kathleen, you look exactly like your dead sister I saw sprawled out on the bed yesterday. The least I could do was figure out where her sister was. I brought the drinks back and handed the mimosa to Kathleen. She accepted thankfully and took a sip through the red and white striped paper straw.

"So, is your sister coming in later?" I asked.

"No, it seems she got a better offer. She texted me late last night."

"When was the last time you talked to her? I mean, what could be more fun than a week down at the beach?" I thought to myself I needed to take it easy and not push too hard. I didn't want to seem too interested.

"Oh, we chat every other day or so. It is a little odd though, because she really loves the beach. But Kaitlyn will be Kaitlyn. I'm sure I will hear from her in the next day or so." She shrugged.

I let it drop for the moment. All the while, Harry was watching this exchange with interest. I changed the subject. "So what floors are everyone staying on?"

Harry said, "Darlene and I are on the floor directly below this on the right as you're looking out at the ocean, and Hanover has got the left."

Kathleen said, "The Crump sisters and I are on the first floor. I think I'm on the left facing the ocean. It actually is very nice being on the first floor because I can walk out to the pool."

The conversation started to drag, and I glanced at others digging into the buffet. "Hey, we should get some of that shrimp and crab cakes before they go."

"I may have one or two of those shrimps, but I'm gonna load up on the crab cakes," said Harry. "Darlene, did you put Tupperware in your purse like I asked you?"

"No Harry, I didn't. You can't possibly think I am going to let you cart off a dozen or so crab cakes. Besides, aren't you supposed to be on a diet?" Darlene said sweetly.

"You see Carlton, this is why you should never get married. Even to my daughter," he said reflectively. "Once they got their hooks in you, they think they can control anything you do."

Darlene just rolled her eyes.

We all wandered over to the buffet and loaded up. Harry got two plates, one for him and one for Darlene. I got a big bowl of the mussels and threw a couple of asiago shrimp and crab cakes on top of that. I had to put my napkin over the top of the bowl and put my hand on top to make sure none of them fell on my way to the back deck. As I passed the Crump sisters, they each had a bowl of salad and a couple of breadsticks. They were standing across from each other, each eating their salad in unison, bite for bite. It looked like I was looking into a mirror with CrumpIT-1 one on one side and CrumpIT-2 on the other. I can't lie to you, I shivered. I nodded and smiled as I went past.

I got out onto the deck and Buddy had beat me to it. He had a salad and some shrimp. He also had a bottle of Miller Light which he was sipping on. I sat down next to him on one of the Phat Tommy chairs. His was turquoise and mine was red. We started talking about the Wright Brothers Memorial.

Buddy was lamenting the fact that Kitty Hawk got credit for the first official flight. "You see, when the Wright Brothers sent word they made their first official flight, it came from the telegraph office located inside the Kitty Hawk Lifesaving Station a few miles away. Kill Devil Hills was not established as an official town until the 1950s, so Kitty Hawk was given the credit as the location of the first flight in 1903 even though the first flight actually took place in Kill Devil Hills." Buddy took another swig of his beer.

A couple of minutes later, Hanover came out followed by Harry and Darlene. We all sat in the chairs, but it didn't take long for Darlene and him to get up and wander to the end of the deck to smoke a cigarette. It must be a known habit because there was a cigarette butt receptacle stand at that end of the deck. I'm sure there was probably one on each floor. I know there was no smoking allowed in the house, but the deck was fair game.

Hanover was kidding Harry about his shirt, saying mine was a whole lot classier.

"That's just a matter of opinion," Harry said stolidly. "Back on the islands, people would come up to me and ask me where I had gotten it."

"Yes, probably to avoid shopping at that store," added Darlene with a straight face. Score one for Darlene.

Everybody laughed. Harry just shook his head.

"Hanover, I have a couple of extras I brought with me. You're more than welcome to borrow one. They are in an overnight bag in one of the spare bedrooms. Feel free to pick one," I said.

"Thanks Carlton, I just might do that."

Buddy wandered back inside for another beer and some crab cakes. He passed Kathleen on the way out. Kathleen put her plate on the rail and stood facing us. I noticed she hadn't drunk much of her mimosa. Hanover looked around to make sure it was just Roger's investors on the back deck before speaking.

"So, Carlton, when are you going to give us the lowdown on what you're really doing down here?"

I laughed. "Hanover, I can understand why you are so popular. You shoot straight from the hip."

Hanover smiled, not really knowing how to take that comment.

I continued. "That does seem to be a topic of discussion doesn't it?" I gave them the party line about being down here to check things out, which I am sure no one actually believed. I'm sure they would rather have had a much more specific definition of 'check things out'. But it wasn't like they could call me a liar, so they let it go. Hanover was going to follow up on the question when Kathleen piped in.

"Carlton, what are your plans for the next couple of days?" she asked questioningly. "I'll bet we're more familiar with this area, and we would love to show you around, wouldn't we?" The rest of the group got the hint and echoed her sentiments.

"I have been down to the Outer Banks before," I said neutrally, "but it's been probably twenty years. I'm sure a lot has changed since then."

"There are plenty of shops," said Kathleen. "And of course there is the Wright Brothers Memorial and the Lost Colony to explore."

Harry was shaking his head. "The man didn't come all the way down here to go shopping and sightseeing. He came down here to enjoy the beach, which is about a hundred feet that way." He pointed to the East.

Darlene said, "There are a number of umbrellas and chairs in the storage room beside the pool downstairs. Maybe we should grab them and set up at the beach tomorrow." That caused pause as everyone thought the idea through, but no one could really find any reason not to. Darlene continued, "We can set up just after high tide which I believe is 8 a.m. tomorrow. Is that right, Harry?" Darlene explained. "Harry has an app for everything on his phone. One for when the garage door goes up, one for when someone passes by the house, one for when our credit cards are used, and he also gets alerts on low and high tides. Sometimes that phone sounds like a pinball machine. I finally told him he had to mute it at night or at least turn it down so I couldn't hear it."

Harry jumped in before Darlene could continue. "Yes, 8 a.m. tomorrow. Actually 8:13 a.m. We can start setting up at the high tide mark, that way we will have a good view of the ocean by ten."

"We can have lunch brought out there," contributed Kathleen.

"Yes, and I have a big cooler we can roll on out there. We have plenty of wine," stated Harry happily.

"Well, I don't think we will be drinking much wine at 10 a.m.," commented Kathleen.

"It is always time to drink wine," scolded Harry playfully. "You know that saying it's five o'clock somewhere? At 10 a.m. tomorrow morning, it's going to be around 5 p.m. in Russia. I'm not saying we need to raise a toast to Russia, but it will be five o'clock there. And we know how much all of them drink." Harry laughed.

Kathleen just rolled her eyes.

"We can get pizza from Slices. I'll even pay for it," said Harry.

"Really? That doesn't sound like you, Harry," said Hanover cautiously.

"No, all I need is your credit card and I'll pay for it. I'll even throw in some hot wings."

"Okay, now that sounds exactly like Harry," said Hanover sourly, turning to me. "Harry is a great big spender"—he paused dramatically—"of other people's money."

"Why don't we get Rhonda to make us a picnic lunch? I'll even pay for it, with my own money," stated Kathleen graciously. "I'm not a tightwad like Harry. I'll go let her know."

"Sounds like a plan," I stated. "I will let the Crump sisters know as well."

"I don't think they'll be coming along," blurted Hanover. "I don't think they are much of a beach crowd."

"Then why did they buy into this house?" I said with a puzzled look.

"Don't get me wrong, I think they like the beach or the beach atmosphere, but I don't see them in two-piece bathing suits frolicking in the water."

I shook my head trying to get that image out of my mind. What would that look like anyway? Synchronized swimming came to mind. "Well, they might surprise you. I will ask them anyway."

"Suit yourself." Hanover shrugged. "But don't be surprised when they turn you down."

Noella Weathers came out and chatted with us. She talked about the new water tower, the latest deaths on the beach, and restaurants that had closed, like American Pie. It was interesting to hear all the local news. Typically, where I live in the Northern Virginia/DC area, all it is about is politics. While there was some of that down here, most of it was actually news. Community news. How the new beach restoration plan was going, roadwork on the Croatan Highway and changes in the recycling station hours. She was funny and gave as good as she got from Harry and Hanover. By that time, I had eaten through my shrimp, crab cakes and mussels. The shrimp was crisp and cheesy on the outside and was moist and flavorful on the inside. The crab cakes were full of crab, not filler. Nice big juicy chunks of crab. I lingered over the mussels and ate them one at a time after I dipped them in the garlic butter.

"Well guys, I am going to go back for another helping." With that I left them talking amongst themselves. I encountered Rhonda on the way back to the buffet, and while I didn't actually gush or ask her to marry me, I let her know how wonderful the food was she had prepared. She seemed generally appreciative and a smile lit up her face. She thanked me warmly and then hurried over to the bar to settle some minor issue. I loaded up again on the mussels, and it looked like everybody else thought it was a big hit as well, since the pile of them had dwindled to an alarmingly low level from the last time I'd grabbed some.

On my way out to the back deck, I stopped to chat with the Crump sisters. "Good evening, ladies."

"Good evening Mr. Russell," said CrumpIt-1.

We didn't get a chance to..." said CrumpIt-2.

"...finish our conversation before," completed CrumpIt-1.

"We will have plenty of time to do that since we are both going to be here over the next couple of days," I said pleasantly. "I was chatting with Hanover, Kathleen, and the Pattersons outside. We are all going to meet up and go to the beach tomorrow morning. We would love to have you be a part of that. Apparently, there are umbrellas and chairs down by the pool."

"Oh yes, certainly. They have..." said CrumpIt-1.

"...a big pavilion tent, which I'm sure between..." said CrumpIt-2.

"...you, Harry and Hanover, can be put up..." said CrumpIt-1.

"...in no time at all," said CrumpIt-2.

Finally, it hit me. I was standing there listening to this verbal ping-pong match when I realized how I could tell the difference between the two of them. I somehow unconsciously made the analogy that when they were standing together earlier it was like looking in a mirror. That was in fact almost literally true because as I watched them now, one was holding her drink in her left hand and the other in her right.

I nodded my head. "You are absolutely right." I then paused because I didn't know who I was saying 'you're absolutely right' to. "I'm sorry, when we were introduced earlier, I wasn't really clear which one of you is Isadora and which is Theodora.

CrumpIt-1 and CrumpIt-2 both blushed. CrumpIt-1 stated, "Most people don't ask because..."

"...they never get it right again afterwards," completed CrumpIt-2. "I'm Isadora and..."

"I'm Theodora," completed Theodora.

"Thank you, I will try to remember it from now on." I mentally made a note that Isadora was left-handed, and Theodora was right-handed and promised to write it down in my notebook before I would forget. "Now, back to tomorrow."

"If you get set up by 8:30 or 9 a.m.," said Isadora.

"...you should get a good spot right out front. Most tourists..." said Theodora.

"...don't show up until about ten or eleven o'clock," nodded Isadora.

"That is really good advice. Sounds like you have done this before." I smiled.

"Not really done it before, but..." said Theodora.

"...we watched from the upstairs balcony," completed Isadora.

"We would be happy if you could join us tomorrow." I said. I was going to continue the she-said-and-she-said back and forth but that is getting a little tiresome. Let's just say every time there is a new line that Isadora completed Theodora's sentence or vice versa.

"I suppose if there are refreshments available..." said Theodora,

"...and the flies aren't biting..."

"...and it's not too hot..."

"...we might be able to stop by for a while."

"Excellent," I exclaimed, switching topics. "Have you tried the mussels? The garlic butter really brings out the flavor in them."

They both shook their heads. "We don't eat..." said Isadora firmly.

"...live creatures."

I said hastily, "Oh no, these have been steamed. So, you don't have to worry about that."

Knowing I had missed the point, Theodora smiled and stated, "No, Mr. Russell, you see…"

"…we are vegetarians."

Now it was my turn to blush from embarrassment. "Oh, got it. Sorry about that. Well, I'm sure there will be something for everyone tomorrow."

Isadora's eyes darted around. Theodora looked around. Isadora said in a whispery tone, "So, I understand you're down here to see…"

"…why Benny and Olaf were killed."

"And Benny was such a nice man. Is that true?" said Isadora.

I partly feigned surprise. I was surprised I got a complete sentence out of one of them but not surprised by the other question. "Where would you hear such a thing?"

"Oh, word gets around," said Isadora loftily.

"And we have very good hearing for our age," added Theodora triumphantly.

"I see, well I can assure you I am not here investigating any individual. Roger merely invited me down," I stated.

Isadora held up her right hand. "Mr. Russell, we know the standard answer you're giving everybody…"

"…but we are just interested in the facts."

Isadora nodded. "We hear all sorts of things and maybe…"

"…some of it might be useful to you."

"We could even be your partners."

"You know, join forces and all."

"Ladies, I can assure you," I started again.

"Did you know the contract we all signed…"

"…has a provision in it…" whispered Theodora.

"…where we could sell our interest to another member?"

"We even received a letter…"

"…asking if we want to sell."

Well that stopped me cold. "Who was the letter from, and when did you get it?" I asked curiously.

"Why Mr. Russell, Theodora said smiling sweetly, "if the only reason…"

"…you are down here is to look the place over…"

"…and have a good time, I don't think there's any reason…"

"…for us to tell you."

"Oh, look Sis, they are putting out…"

"…those little chocolate drops we adore."

"We'll be talking later,"

"Mr. Russell."

And with that the Crump sisters left and went over to examine the dessert tray. I stood there, part irritated and part in admiration at how easily I'd been outmaneuvered by those two. Well this certainly added a new wrinkle to the problem.

I went back out to the deck, but everyone had left except Harry and Darlene. Harry finished his cigarette and came over to me.

"So, what do you think?"

Darlene looked puzzled. I looked puzzled and turned to Harry. "What do I think about what?"

"Which one of them killed them?"

"Harry! You can't go around accusing people of things like that," exclaimed Darlene.

"I'm not accusing anybody. I was just asking if Mr. Carlton Russell was accusing anybody."

"I think you are kinda jumping the gun here, Harry. Not investigating anybody, and not accusing anybody. Besides, there are four other investors I haven't even met yet."

"Oh, them," Harry said disgustingly. "Once you meet them you will know they are light weights compared with these people. Why do you think they got the second week?"

"Well, I won't know until I talk to them. Besides, maybe you are the killer," I said coolly.

That got a loud laugh out of Harry. "That's a hot one. Although there are times when I would love to get my hands around Kathleen's neck and —" Harry stopped and sipped his wine.

"Harry! You need to stop talking like that or Mr. Russell is going to take you seriously," scolded Darlene. "Harry sometimes gets a little careless with his words," she explained.

"Baa, Darlene, I say exactly what I mean to say. Heck, Carlton, even I picked up on an interesting fact this evening that can't be explained and got me thinking."

"Oh, would you care to share?"

"Well, I never give away information for free. Besides, right now it is just a hunch. I will let you know if it becomes more valuable," Harry said smugly.

I should have pushed and gotten the information out of Harry. Even if I had to pay for it. But hindsight is 20/20, as they say.

Harry was about to say something when he spied the dessert cart through the open doors. "Darlene, didn't Rhonda say she was going to fix some of those miniature Shoney's Hot Fudge Cakes?" Harry licked his lips. "I do love my Shoney Hot Fudge Cakes. Come on Darlene, I want to get one before they are all gone." With that, Harry and Darlene left, leaving me alone to think about what he'd said. And more importantly, what he hadn't.

After the horde of locusts descended on the dessert tray, the party broke up. Noella and Buddy said their goodbyes and everybody else descended in the elevator to their respective floors. I looked around and the crowd had done a pretty good job at demolishing all the food, although there was still a good supply of alcohol. That's not to say no one drank; there was a pretty healthy supply there before the party started. I did note that two bottles of Woodbridge were empty.

"So how did we do tonight?" inquired Rhonda as she walked around.

"I think it was an excellent shindig," I said enthusiastically.

Rhonda smiled. "You mean soirée, right?"

I laughed. "I can't get anything over on you, can I?"

"Not when you toss words around like soirée and shindig. No, seriously, any suggestions? I'm always interested in feedback, good or bad."

"I think it was fabulous. I wouldn't change a thing. Oh, did Kathleen talk to you about lunch tomorrow?"

"Yes, I think I'll do some barbeque and cookies, homemade of course. Also, I'll add in some fresh lemonade."

"I think the Crump sisters are going to be there as well, so make sure you have some vegetarian wraps."

"Really? They usually don't attend extracurricular functions. You must have put a spell on them."

"That is because I'm a consummate flirt and I swept them off their feet."

"Ooh, I see I am not the only one here with a good memory."

I grinned. The other two caterers were starting to break everything down. "Say, any chance I could save a couple of those shrimps and crab cakes? You never know when I'll have a craving for them at 2 a.m. in the morning."

"Sure, I'll have them wrap it up and put it in the refrigerator for you along with your Gray Goose. I better get to work to get everything broken down to get out of here at a reasonable hour. That way we can get out of your hair."

"Oh, I'm not at all sleepy, I think I'll go for a drive. If you just lock up when you leave, that would be great."

"Sure, it looks like I'll see you tomorrow."

I smiled and nodded. "Until then." I grabbed my car keys and went down in the elevator and out to the car. I looked around and it was all quiet except for the sound of the ocean. Little wisps of cloud floated overhead, and the stars were putting on a spectacular show. Being my normal paranoid self, I took a left out of the parking lot and drove down Beach Road for about half a mile. I turned right on St. Clair Street and turned right again to get on Croatan Highway. I turned right on East Landing and a left on Sir Walter Road. I kept glancing in the rear-view mirror, but no cars seemed to have any interest in where I was going.

I parked at the cottage and went inside and fixed myself a V&T. I went out on the back deck and could hear the ocean in the distance. I mulled, if mulled is the word I am looking for. Kathleen's appearance, Harry's opinions and guesses, the Crumps, and the letters. It was a lot to take in. How did they all connect, or did they? Was Kathleen's twin sister really dead? I thought so, but if that's true, where's the body? Who sent all the mysterious texts from her phone?

What did Harry know that I didn't? There was something devious about Harry, and I didn't know if that was a good or bad thing. I could easily see him as the one behind those letters. But then again it could have been one of the others I hadn't met yet. Maybe they were making a play for an equity stake in the house. Knock off a couple of investors, buy off the rest and then you could squeeze Roger out of the house, and he'd be forced to sell.

What secrets did the Crump sisters know? Did they know who was sending the letters?

The only ones that didn't seem to have any questions surrounding them were Hanover and Darlene. Somehow that didn't make me feel any more comfortable about them. Maybe they were just better at hiding what they were doing.

I finished the V&T and felt tired. I'd learned a lot but didn't know anything.

Chapter 6

I woke up the next morning to the sound of my cell phone ringing. I hit the snooze button and rolled back over in bed. About two minutes later, the phone rang again. I realized the phone was not going to stop ringing until I answered it. I sat up in bed and did so.

"This is CR. Good morning. How can I help you?" I said in a grouchy tone.

"Good morning, sunshine. You know if you change locations you should probably leave a forwarding address or let people know so they can get a hold of you rather than track you down."

I recognized the voice immediately as E. "Good morning E, what can I do for you on this bright and extremely early morning?" I said in a sleepy monotone voice. For those that remember, E was short for Esmeralda Francesca Guadalupe Zara Gonzales. Flavia recommended her after

Natalie blew up my townhouse. She was supposed to be very good but was also very annoying. Apparently, she was brushing up on her annoying skills that morning.

"I just wanted to give you a quick update on everything," she said, ignoring my tone. "I sent in all the paperwork with the insurance company. They aren't particularly happy about it, but they are going to pony up the money to cover the replacement costs. Of course, that will probably be four to six weeks down the road before I see a check on that. I was able to get everything squared away with the county and got a building permit. I also was able to locate the builder who built this gem of a townhouse. Are you sure you want me to put everything back the way it was?"

"What's wrong with the way it was?"

"Dude, this thing was built in the 70s. Times have changed since then."

"Oh, and how have they changed?"

"ADA, Americans with Disabilities Act. You know, make things wider and more accessible. If you ever think of selling the townhouse, you're probably going to get a set of old folks in there who are going to want to be able to push their wheelchairs around. How are they going to be able to do that with those narrow-ass doorways and all those steps? Also, we got this thing now called open spaces people like and Feng Shui. I know you want to have your energy forces to harmonize with your surrounding environment. Plus, you want to be able to see from one end of the house to the other. Don't want to miss any action going on in the other rooms.

You got everything all chopped up in there. It's a wonder you can move around without hitting a wall or a door."

"E, do whatever you think is right."

"Are you kidding me? Is that the sleep talking, or do you really mean it? Because if you actually mean that, I'm off and running. But don't you go coming back later on and saying I told you so or you want something different, because you just now gave me permission to do what I want. I am going to Feng the Shui out of the house. You do know I'm going to send you a follow-up email to confirm this conversation and you will have to confirm?"

"Yes, yes, I'm sure you'll be guided by your intelligence and experience," I quoted sagely but in a tired voice.

"Good grief, what is that? Some type of psychological mumbo-jumbo? I think I like you better when you're fully awake. Anyway, we are ordering materials and supplies and will get started by the end of the week. I figured you wouldn't want an outdated floorplan, so I already revised them to get it where it needs to be. Oh, and I think we already got your neighbor problem solved."

"My neighbor has a problem?"

"No, our problem with your neighbor. More correctly stated, your problem with your neighbor. You know, Wild Bill Knittel. The one packing a 45. I seriously thought him and Carlos were going to get out in the middle of the street at noon and have a showdown. Anyway, we won't have to worry about Mr. and Mrs. Knittel for at least the next couple of weeks."

"Oh, did you arrest them and put them in jail?"

"No!" She laughed. "I did one better than that."

"Drop them in a big hole and cover it up?"

"Nope, I sent them on a cruise?"

"I beg your pardon. You did what?"

E laughed again. "Yup, I packed their asses up and sent them on a cruise. I told them in my sweetest voice and most convincing smile it was impossible to find such wonderful and understanding neighbors as them. This was your way of making it up to them. All they had to do was to pick the place and off they would go."

"Ah huh."

"So right about now they are heading down to Florida to jump on that big old cruise ship. They're scheduled for a four-week tour of the Caribbean. We won't see their asses back here until we are ready to lay carpet. Incidentally, we're not laying carpet. Hardwood all throughout the house."

"I see, and how much is this going to cost me?"

E really couldn't contain her enthusiasm over this. "Well the other night I was home, and I was flipping through this travel magazine and I saw this coupon, and that's what gave me the idea. I didn't know they had coupons for cruises. Anyway, I clipped it out and took it in and showed it to Flavia.

"And let me guess," I said sarcastically, now being fully awake. "She thought it was a wonderful idea."

"Ain't that the truth. She couldn't wait to give the travel agency a call and book their flights and cruise with your corporate credit card. I'm not sure how she got your credit card number, but she has it and she was more than happy to whip it out and give it to them."

Yes, on every corporate credit card I have, I'm obligated to pay any charges that are made on it that are not reimbursed by the company. I can only guess this will be one of those.

"I think she even threw in a couple hundred dollars in cruise credits," continued E. "That's money you can spend while on board for drinks and doodads in the gift shop."

"Great, simply great," I said dryly. "I can't wait to have a little chat with Flavia about that,"

"Yes indeed, I couldn't believe it. I have never seen Flavia smile and laugh so much as when she was booking those tickets. You would think she was possessed by the devil."

Truer words were never spoken, I thought to myself. I gritted my teeth. "I got it. How about you call me when you actually have done some real work and got my townhouse rebuilt."

"Oh, I see somebody hasn't had their first cup of coffee this morning."

I looked at my cell for the time and it was 6:12 a.m. "E, nobody has had their first cup of coffee this early in the morning." I disconnected the phone call by jabbing the end call button. I miss the old days where I could slam down the telephone receiver and it would make a jarring noise that could be heard on the other end of the line. I sighed, oh the good old days.

I could only imagine what that trip was going to cost me, but in a weird sort of way, it did make sense. Although I really hated the fact Flavia was going to get a lot of mileage out of this one. I could just see her in her office, cackling and laughing over my misfortune. I mentally added in a cauldron, broom, and her wearing a black pointed hat. That at least gave me a little satisfaction.

I tried to get back to sleep but it wasn't going to happen. I got up and fixed some breakfast. The eggs I'd bought were farm fresh and cost twice as much as a regular egg, but you can really taste the difference in the flavor, and the yolk was a lot more orange than yellow. I like my eggs over easy but not so easy that the whites are running. The English muffins I got were Bay English muffins. You don't find them in the bread aisle. They are tucked in near the eggs and cheese. When I first tried them, they didn't feel like they were anything special. But after they were toasted with a generous helping of butter added, they are heaven on earth. Crunchy and chewy at the same time with a delightful flavor. I finished it off with a thick slice of Spam. The muffins were toasting, the eggs were cooking, and the Spam was sizzling. All was right with the world.

I ate out on the back deck. I checked the forecast and it said there would be some light rain in the morning, but the afternoon was going to turn out to be nice. I didn't see any evidence of the rain, but in the Outer Banks sometimes the rain sneaks up on you. I finished eating and went back inside to cleanup, paying particular attention to the cast-iron. I washed it gently with warm water and applied a light coat of oil to it and rubbed it down until it was dry. Everything else went in the dishwasher.

I drove back over to the house. I showered and changed into some appropriate beach attire. I went through the whole floor to ensure there weren't any surprises. There weren't. I looked outside and saw there was some activity on the beach out front, so I went down to help set up. Harry and Hanover had already dragged out most of the chairs and the pavilion. Harry was directing how to set everything up. The chairs were arranged in a semicircle facing the beach. There was a long low table in front of that which I assumed we would put our drinks on. Harry had hauled down his cooler on wheels and placed it near his chairs. The light rain had started, and the wind had picked up from the east.

Chapter 7

I DUCKED BACK UNDERNEATH the deck to stay out of the rain. Kathleen came up. "Looks like you're all set up."

"Yes, now if the rain would just cooperate and go away, it would be a fairly nice day."

"The pavilion will keep the rain off. But the wind is carrying it up and down the beach."

We went through some more chitchat, but I felt she had something else she wanted to say.

"Carlton, I understand you're down here to figure out if there are any issues. But I really think Roger is on the wrong track."

"Oh, why do you think that? What about Benny and Olaf?"

Kathleen shrugged. "Just coincidences. They happen all the time. Roger tends to see ghosts and goblins at every turn."

"Maybe," I said. "But it doesn't hurt to take a couple of days to check it out." I looked around at the misty rain and wind. "Well, except for days like this."

"I checked with the weather channel before I came out, and this is supposed to end in the next hour. Then it will be sunny the rest of the day. Don't worry." She patted my arm." You will get what you came here for. But I think you really are wasting your time. I'm sure there's someone or something back home that needs more of your attention."

"Why Kathleen," I said with my best disarming smile, "don't you like it that I'm here?" Her answer was interrupted by my phone ringing. I looked at the caller ID and it was Natalie. "Listen, I've got to take this call, but I will see you back here in sunnier times." I walked back into the house and punched in the keycode for the top floor. By the time I got up there, the call had been forwarded to my voicemail. I hit redial and heard her phone ringing. She picked up on the second ring.

"Hey there CR, I was just leaving you a message."

"Sorry, I was in an elevator. So, what is up, my dear?"

"I am an hour away."

"An hour away from what?"

"From the cottage, silly."

"You mean you're almost down here?"

"Well sure. I was going to wait another day or two but the thought of being able to stretch out on the beach was just too much for me."

My mind shifted gears. "Okay, I am out running errands at the moment and I've got a commitment for a beach party late this morning and this afternoon."

"Oh, I love beach parties," she said enthusiastically. "It will give me a chance to try out my new swim attire."

"By attire, I assume you mean swimsuit."

"Among other things," she said mysteriously.

"Yes, I'm sure that will be fun," I said weakly. "I'll meet you at the cottage in about an hour. If you get there before me, the key is under the mat upstairs."

"Tootles, see you in an hour."

For a second my mind took a sharp right turn. I wonder if Natalie knew that tootles was the anglicized pronunciation of the French saying *"à tout à l'heure"* which meant see you later. This I learned from a discussion with Reynolds a couple of months ago when he talked about words and phrases that had taken on new meanings. I shook my head to clear my thoughts and get them back on track. I hung up and thought a moment and concluded this might not be a bad thing.

Natalie was a natural inquisitive mixer. And I'm sure she could draw out these people to talk more about themselves, which may reveal information they might not otherwise say to me. The more I thought about it, the better I liked it. I hung around for another half hour or so until the rain stopped. I went back down to the ground floor and was heading for the parking lot when I bumped into Hanover.

"Just checking to see if the wind and the rain had messed up what we set up earlier," he said pleasantly.

"I have a couple of errands I have to run but will be back within the hour. I am going to be bringing a friend who just popped down for a couple of days."

"I'll make sure we set out another chair."

I could tell he was dying to ask more but knew he would get his answers when I came back. I took the long route again back to the cottage, not wanting anybody to know I stayed there. I got there and tidied up and about twenty minutes later, Natalie rolled up in a new Chrysler 300. She jumped out and gave me a hug.

"I see you are still living off the generosity of others. Having your license suspended doesn't seem to have stopped you from driving," I exclaimed.

"That was only in Virginia, this is North Carolina. I feel like I have been given a new lease on life."

"You do know that's not how it works, right?"

She just stuck her tongue out at me.

"Whose car is this? Or did you steal it right off the lot?"

"My goodness, we are just full of piss and vinegar today, aren't we? Well, if you must know, it's Walter's."

"Walter?"

"Honestly CR, sometimes I think you don't pay attention to a word I say. Walter Dittmar. The plants I was taking care of, his dear dog Trouble, ring a bell?"

"Dear dog Trouble?" I raised my eyebrows but let that pass. "Oh, so Walter allowed you to take his practically new

Chrysler 300 for a joy ride to North Carolina? Besides, your license is still suspended, isn't it?"

"Yes, but not in North Carolina!" she said in an exasperated tone. "Walter, I am sure would have said it was okay if he was around. But it just so happens he is out of the country for a couple of weeks. I'm sure he wouldn't mind," she concluded hastily.

"Ah huh. All right, let's get you inside."

Natalie went to the trunk of the Chrysler and pulled out a humongous suitcase.

"You didn't tell me you were moving down here," I said, eyeing the suitcase. "You are only going to be here for a couple of days, aren't you?"

"Well, of course silly, but it's not like I can run back to my apartment if I need something." Natalie smiled brightly. "So, I brought everything I might need."

I eyed the suitcase again. "I think you have all your bases covered." I huffed and I puffed as I dragged it up the front steps and into the cottage.

Natalie ooh-ed and aah-ed over the cottage and said it was very quaint and romantic. She loved the bathroom bowl sink that was shaped like a fish, and all the local artwork. I pointed to a room at the back of the house. "That's where I've got my stuff, so you can fill up the other three rooms with yours."

She punched me on the arm. "It's not like I'm going to unpack everything in my suitcase," she said with her hands on her hips and her eyebrows raised. She then dragged her stuff to the nearest bedroom and started unpacking her essentials.

I could hear her humming 'Somewhere Over the Rainbow' and so told Alexa to play songs from the Wizard of Oz. It started out loudly with 'If I Only Had a Brain.' I hastily turned it off. "Alexa play songs by Israel Ka'ano'i Kamakawiwo'ole." It took me about six months to say his name right so Alexa would understand it. The song White Sandy Beach started playing. Much more to my liking.

Natalie popped her head out of the bedroom about fifteen minutes later.

"You mentioned something about a party? I'm ready."

I looked outside. The sun was peeking out from the clouds and I looked out to the east and it was clear. "We can go anytime now," I said.

She jumped out of the room as if it was one of those ta-da moments, arms and legs akimbo, and she twirled around. I wished I got that on camera. It looked like her bathing suit had been spray-painted on and very little paint had been used. She had on a bright blue thong bikini with a postage-stamp top. Actually, it took a couple of postage stamps and an air mail stamp to cover up properly. Over that she was wearing a loose electric yellow beach cover-up. She had on what looked like platform shoes, Ray Ban sunglasses and a floppy straw sun hat. I am not sure what all she had in her suitcase, but she could have put the bathing suit in my wallet.

I went up to her and wrapped my arms around her.

"Easy on the merchandise, tiger. It hasn't been paid for or tested yet."

I whispered in her ear. "Maybe I can't afford to buy it, but can I rent it for an hour or two?"

She laughed and pushed me away. "No, the cover-up, my handsome Lothario."

I gave her a puzzled look.

"This little gem is supposed to be the newest thing in smart wear. And I am reviewing it," she said holding out the cover-up.

"Okay, you'll have to forgive me if I didn't notice the cover-up," I said dryly. "My mind was slightly preoccupied with the bathing suit, or lack thereof it.".

She grinned. "Good answer."

"Don't you think you're going to catch cold in an outfit like that?"

"Well there are suits for swimming and there are suits for sunbathing and there are suits for driving men crazy. This one falls under the third category. She said with a mischievous glint in her eyes. "Catching a cold is sometimes the price you pay." She went over, rummaged around in her suitcase, and then asked, "DO you have any sunscreen?"

I got a wide-eyed look on my face. "What, no sunscreen? I guess there wasn't enough room in that big suitcase over yonder to fit an itty-bitty bottle of sunscreen?"

She blushed. "Well, you can't think of everything."

I had mercy on her. "Yes, in that cabinet on your left there is a wide assortment of sunscreen that apparently were left by other renters.

She opened the cabinet and selected some SPF 30 and some Maui Babe Browning Lotion.

"You are such a tease," I exclaimed.

"What?" She looked at me innocently.

"You know exactly what I'm talking about. We are going to get down to the beach and you are going to ask me in your softest seductive innocent voice if I couldn't possibly put some Maui Babe on you. You know, every male on the beach is going to turn and look at me doing that with their tongues hanging out. Many a girlfriend and wife are going to hate you, and you are going to love it."

She pouted. "You know CR, sometimes you're just no fun!"

"Yeah, that's me, a party pooper."

She reluctantly put the Maui Babe back.

I grabbed my car keys, and we went over to the house. On the way over there, I explained I was working on a project with a friend and he had lent me the top floor of the house.

"Then why are you staying in this cottage?" she asked.

That was a really good question. I didn't want to explain to her that if I stayed in the house, I might end up dead, so I improvised. "I had already rented the cottage down here, plus all the other residents of the house can use that upper floor as an entertaining area in the evenings." That sounded plausible to me.

Natalie stared at me. "CR, what are you not telling me?"

Okay, plausible to me but apparently not to Natalie. I looked at her innocently. "What? Nothing."

She sighed. "Okay, just tell me the lie I am supposed to tell."

"For all they know I live on the top floor. They don't need to know I have a cottage where I spend my nights."

We went in and I punched the code for the top floor. The doors opened and she came into the room and just sighed. "Oh CR, are you sure we can't stay here?" she said wistfully. She walked over to the bank of windows looking out to the pool and ocean, her platform heels clicking loudly on the hardwood floor. "What a view!"

"We can stay here during the day but at night we turn into pumpkins and go back to the cottage."

"Well, we will just make do with what we have." She walked out onto the deck and looked out. "Oh, is that where the party is?" she said, pointing to the pavilion.

I walked out and stood beside her. "Yes, that's it. I will introduce you to everybody when we get down there. Now you be a good girl and be on your best behavior."

She laughed wickedly. "Yes master!"

"Wait a minute, was that Young Frankenstein?"

Natalie just batted her eyelashes.

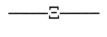

Chapter 8

WE GOT DOWNSTAIRS and out to the pavilion. Harry and Darlene were already there. Harry was standing there ogling Natalie with his mouth open as we approached.

I whispered to Natalie. "That's Harry and Darlene Patterson."

As Natalie got closer, she squealed. "Harry, Harry Patterson, oh my God it's been so long. But I forgive you. Even though you didn't call afterwards." She ran up and gave him a big hug. I just stood there and groaned.

Harry looked like a trapped animal. He darted glances between Darlene and Natalie. I knew for a fact Natalie had never met Harry before. But leave it up to her to have a dramatic entrance.

Natalie pulled away as she held Harry's hands and looked Harry up and down. "So how is my big stud muffin doing?" She paused. "Wait a minute. That was Harvey

Patterson, not Harry. I am so sorry. He walked with a limp. Do you have a limp by any chance? No, probably not. Well, that's too bad." She sighed reluctantly. "Harvey had a really big"—pausing to eye Harry up and down—"heart. But it is good to meet you anyway. I'm Natalie by the way."

Harry stammered. "And this is my wife Darlene."

Darlene's eyes looked like they could bore through solid steel as she looked from Harry to Natalie. "Harry, who is this woman and where did you meet her?"

"Honestly Darlene, I've never met her before," Harry said defensively as he looked appreciatively at Natalie. "I am quite sure that is something I would remember. Although she does look a little bit like that dancer at Headlights, but this one has a lot more curves. A lot more."

That resulted in a smack from Darlene. I decided it was time to step in and slow things down a bit. Oh, in case you haven't been down to the Outer Banks, Headlights is an adult entertainment club. Okay, it is a strip club and is located on the right,before you cross over the Wright Memorial Bridge into the Outer Banks. One of my new friends at Goombays had even suggested their chicken pot pie was pretty good. Needless to say, I didn't put it on my must-eat-at list. "Don't worry Harry, Natalie routinely mistakes people for somebody else." I guided Natalie away from them and over to the drink table.

"What was that about?" I whispered furiously.

Natalie giggled. "I could tell as soon as we came down here, he was giving me the eye. You know, where they are mentally undressing you. So, I figured two could play that game. I'll bet Darlene thinks twice about letting him go to Headlights again. It doesn't look like she's going to let him too far out of sight for a long while anyway." She laughed.

I stared at her. "You are one evil woman. I'm certainly glad you're on my side."

"Hmmmm."

"You are on my side, right?" I questioned.

Natalie just smiled. "Oh look, more guests have arrived."

Good Lord, what had I unleashed on this crowd? Rhonda's crew had apparently come out earlier and laid out some lemonade, juices, bottled water, and sodas. I grabbed a Diet Coke and Natalie got a fresh squeezed lemonade.

Hanover, Kathleen, and the Crump sisters all arrived as a group. I glanced over at Harry and Darlene and they were having an animated conversation. I was pretty sure Harry was on the losing end of it. When Natalie introduced herself to Hanover, he glanced quickly over me and gave me a quick nod as if to indicate attaboy. The Crump sisters were a lot more stoic, and you could see disapproval written all over their faces at the way Natalie was dressed or rather not dressed. Of course, they were dressed so that practically none of their skin was shown, where Natalie was the opposite.

Everybody moved under the pavilion and went to the drink table. After everyone had gotten their drink of choice, Kathleen commented on Natalie's cover-up.

"Oh, this is one of my items I am evaluating."

Everyone looked puzzled. I interjected. "Natalie runs a pretty popular blog called Natalie's Tricks and Treats. She gets various manufacturers to send her products to test out and then she writes about them."

By this time Harry and Darlene had wandered over to hear the conversation. "Holy cow, you're the one that did the review on the grasshopper," Harry exclaimed before realizing he had said it out loud. That brought another glare from Darlene, and the next comment he was about to make died on his lips.

I hurried on. "She brought down a couple of items to try out at the beach and it looks like this is one of them."

All eyes turned back to Natalie. "This is called a smart cover-up."

"And what is it supposed to be smart about?" I asked, playing her straight man.

"Well," Natalie said warming to the subject, "there are little cameras in the shoulders—you can hardly see them—and there's a speaker in the pocket down below, or you can use a wireless earbud. It uses some type of facial recognition software and it's connected to an app on your phone. You can tell who is approaching."

"Why would I need a shirt for that? Couldn't I just look at the person?" questioned Hanover.

"Yes, I guess if you want to do it that way, but this provides you a whole lot more detail about the person. With this you can even associate the face with facts. For example, if your boss's wife is coming toward you and you don't remember her name, it will tell you that and her kids names, where she went to high school, and even her favorite foods."

"What happens to the people it doesn't recognize or to people who don't want to be recognized?" inquired Kathleen.

That's the thing," Natalie said excitedly. "They don't even know it's happening. The cover-up grabs a picture of the person, sends it to the phone, the phone does a search of the Internet to find a compatible picture, and bingo, you now know who you're talking to. Oh, and here is a cool feature, based on your picture it will pick the closest personality type and express it as a song. Here, let me demonstrate." She tapped a couple commands on her cell phone and turned to face me.

Two seconds passed before the song *Love to Love You Babe* by Donna Summer started blaring out of her pocket. Everyone laughed while I turned red. Next, she turned to Harry, almost immediately the song switched to *Hey There Little Red Riding Hood* by Sam the Sham and the Pharaohs. She turned to Kathleen who looked a little uncomfortable. The song switched to the theme from the Twilight Zone. Everyone blinked at that one. "Huh, that is odd. I have never seen it do that before," said Natalie in a perplexed tone. She instantly turned to Hanover. Everyone quickly identified the theme song from Top Gun. Natalie pulled her cell phone out again to turn the cover-up off. Everybody clapped in delight. Natalie bowed.

Natalie floated around chatting with everybody. She even got the Crump sisters to talk to her. Of course, Hanover and Harry followed her around like puppy dogs, which was to be expected. I noticed after a while she had a good conversation with Kathleen and had made nice-nice with Darlene. Natalie was quite the diplomat when she wanted to be. Unfortunately, that was an unpredictable trait in her.

It was starting to get to be towards lunch time and I noticed Rhonda and her crew had just showed up. They had set up two tables at the edge of the pavilion and one had boxes on it for lunches. Each box had one of our names on it. They stashed away half of the drinks and put in a minibar. Well by minibar, it was about half the size of the bar last night, but it still had quite a variety of drinks including my V&T ingredients. Apparently, the bartender had paid attention to what people drank because instead of a whole array of wines I saw only Woodbridge and Kendall Jackson Chardonnay.

There was my Gray Goose chilling in a bucket, a bottle of champagne chilling in another bucket, and a pitcher of orange juice next to it. Rhonda greeted me with a smile.

"Mr. Carlton Russell, we meet again. I am so happy to see you."

"And I am happy to see you." I said warmly. "I'm glad you're able to grace us with your presence,"

"Well as I tell everybody, I may be easy but I'm not cheap. Or is it the other way around?" she said frowning.

I laughed. "Either way, it'll make it effortless for you to get a second date."

She laughed with me and looked around at the crowd, and her eyes settled on Natalie. Her eyebrows raised and she looked at me. "One of yours?" she asked questioningly with an amused smile on her face.

"What do you mean by that 'one of yours' crack?" I said feigning to be offended. "She just happened to be down, and I just happened to invite her."

"Sure, and the pope just happened to be Catholic. Is there anything I should know about her?"

"Oh, jealous?" I said playfully.

"In terms of eats and drinks, Romeo."

"Oh," I said, appropriately taken down a peg or two. "Natalie will pretty much drink or eat anything. She is just like a Tasmanian devil if you put her in front of a buffet. I can't understand how she keeps her figure like that."

As I said that last statement, Harry had walked up to get a refill on his wine. "You talking about Natalie? I know exactly how she keeps her figure, lots of sex. Sex, sex, sex. I'll bet she can bend like a pretzel," said Harry as his eyes glazed over envisioning the thought. "Yessiree, that'll burn off the calories. You get to know that type when you own an adult video store like I did."

"I thought you sold insurance?" questioned Rhonda.

"Oh, the adult video store was before. You wouldn't believe all of the people that came in there. From schoolteachers to priests. They were all looking for the same thing. That's right. Sex!"

Rhonda laughed. "Mr. Patterson, not everybody has your obsession for sex."

"They don't?" Harry said as a look of surprise crossed his face. "Well if they don't, they should." He winked at her and grabbed his glass of wine on his way back to where Darlene was sitting.

I just shook my head.

Rhonda said, "I do believe he was the one who came up with the idea that the theme for the cocktail party last night should be French and the caterers should all dress in French maid outfits. Even the guys. When I told Lucas about it," she said pointing over to a beefy looking gentleman setting up the barbecue, "he threatened to quit on the spot."

"I agree," I said supportively. "A man should never dress up in a maid outfit, although if you replaced him with another woman..." I paused, mulling it over.

Rhonda just rolled her eyes. "You're as bad as the rest of them."

I grinned. "It's a liability of the gender."

Natalie had by now noticed us talking and wandered over to introduce herself.

"Natalie, this is Rhonda. She is the hostess with the mostest and has a catering company here in town."

Natalie hit a button on her cell phone and from her pocket there blared the song, *Born to be Wild* by Steppenwolf. Rhonda and I both jumped at the sudden onslaught of music. Natalie hit another button on her cell phone and the music suddenly stopped.

Natalie smiled sweetly and shook Rhonda's hand. "I am so happy to meet you. My, my, it looks like I am definitely going to have to keep my eye on you." She smiled again and asked for and received a glass of champagne, no orange juice, and wandered off to talk to Hanover.

Rhonda's eyes got big. "What was that all about?"

I sighed. "Are you really sure you want to know?"

She nodded her head, so I related the whole story with full orchestration and three-part harmony about the smart cover-up and the songs that were selected for everybody. I'll admit I blushed a little bit when I told her the song selected for me.

When she heard that, she let out a laugh. "I knew I should have gotten here earlier," she said, shaking her head.

I went over to a table and retrieved the box that had my name on it and opened it. It was empty except for some plastic utensils and napkins. I looked at Rhonda questioningly.

"I could say it was a metaphor for hunger in America, but what it really means is everyone gets a box and can fill it up with anything from the table Lucas is setting up. You have to be patient—we'll be finished setting up soon. We figured it was the best way to serve food on the beach. That way the flies don't get to it. And besides, it's easier to clean up."

The Crump sisters wandered up and asked Rhonda if she had any sparkling water. I went over to look at the food. Lucas had just finished laying out beef brisket, pulled pork, four different kinds of barbecue sauce, two different kinds of coleslaw, potato rolls, and chicharrons. For dessert they had small bags of kettle corn and little boxes of what looked to be snickerdoodle cookies. My stomach was doing a happy dance in anticipation.

As soon as everyone saw Lucas had finished setting up, they all grabbed their boxes and lined up as Rhonda explained what was being served. She also pointed to two salads which were specially prepared for the Crump sisters. Rhonda had provided a couple of extra boxes in anticipation of others showing up, and Natalie grabbed one of those. She wrote her name on it with a magic marker.

When it got to be my turn, I was strategic and got two barbecue sandwiches, one beef and one pork. I figured I would have a little extra room in the box because I didn't put any kettle corn or cookies in it. I could go back for them later.

I sat at a table with Harry, Darlene and Hanover. Natalie sat with Kathleen and the Crump sisters. I saw Natalie had carried over a bottle of champagne to her table and was filling up cups for everybody, including herself. At our table, Harry and Hanover were having an animated discussion, and I tried to keep track of whether Harry interrupted Hanover more than Hanover interrupted Harry. After the first couple of minutes it was pretty evenly split. The conversation seemed to be focused on the downfall of men who ran around with cheating women.

"A lot of these women fall into the same category," exclaimed Harry.

I fell for it. "And what would that be?"

"These men all ran around with short women."

I did a double take. "Short women?"

"Yup, that is a scourge on this earth, short women. Every time I have had a relationship with a short woman, it has ended in disaster. They can be the most needy, bitchy, demanding people on the face of this planet. Why, I told my son Harry Junior that exact thing before he married that first wife of his, Susan. I said Harry Junior, this is going to end badly for you. It ain't gonna last. When he asked why, I said because she's short," Harry concluded triumphantly.

Hanover and I were little dumbfounded by this philosophy. Darlene continued to eat her coleslaw and barbecue. Out of the corner of my eye, I could see Rhonda edging closer so she could hear the conversation better. She was relishing every word of it and I'm sure it would be repeated the moment she walked out, although she was a little torn because there was a lot of laughter coming from the other table. Natalie, I'm sure was relating one of her stories. My guess was she was telling everyone how my townhouse blew up.

Harry paused and sipped his wine. He took a bite of the barbecue and then some coleslaw. We all sat there waiting for, as Paul Harvey would say, the rest of the story. When I couldn't take it any longer, I said, "And?"

Harry looked up confused from his barbecue. "And what?"

"And did it last, you idiot?" exclaimed Hanover in a frustrated voice.

"Oh, that," Harry said with a smug smile, knowing exactly the dramatic effect he had caused. "Naw, in a year they were both in divorce court and he was dumping her by the side of the road. But get this, Harry Junior then hooks up with another woman who wasn't much taller than the first one. Sometimes I think my boy has got a bag of doorknobs for brains."

Darlene had put up with this monologue for a while, and I'm sure it wasn't the first time she'd heard that story. "Harry, don't you go talking trash about Martha."

"I'm just saying," said Harry, "she's a little taller than the first one, but she's still pretty short. I'd give them a fifty-fifty chance."

"Harry, when Martha comes over to the house, she cooks for you and she helps me clean and she's good to our Harry." Darlene said defensively. "I couldn't think of a better daughter-in-law."

"I don't know," grumbled Harry. "I think it's a ploy and she's just waiting to spring her shortness on him. And besides, that woman gets me to spend money."

"What do you mean, spend money?" asked Darlene. "They've never asked us for a penny."

"What do you call that new outdoor furniture?" Harry turned to Hanover and me. "She told me my old outdoor furniture looked like the waiting room at the city dump. Can you imagine that?"

I turned to Darlene. "Did it look like the waiting room at the city dump?"

Darlene didn't wait for the question to be asked twice before she was all over it. She nodded her head vigorously. "I was afraid to invite people over," she stated confidentially. "Not only was the furniture hideous, nothing matched, and I thought if someone sat down on a chair, they would fall right through to the ground."

"Oh Darlene, it wasn't that bad."

"That stuff was about to fall apart, and you knew it, Harry. All Martha did was point out the obvious."

"Well, it could have lasted another year or two if she hadn't interfered," grumbled Harry as he shook his head. "Now she is working to get rid of my recliner. There are limits you know. Short women, I'm telling ya, nothing but trouble."

"So, did you get new outdoor furniture?" I asked.

"Did I ever!" She said gaily. "When Harry Patterson cracks open his wallet, you make sure you take it to the limit because you never know when that's going to happen again."

Harry just looked sour and took a big swig of his wine.

Lunch ended and I snuck back over and grabbed a couple of bags of kettle corn and boxes of snickerdoodles. Everybody went out into the sun to relax after the meal. I noticed Natalie had gotten Hanover to spray on her SPF and make sure it was rubbed into her bronze skin. She looked over at me looking at her and scrunched her nose into a triumphant smirk. I just rolled my eyes.

I looked over and saw Harry was mesmerized by the application of the SPF.

"Darlene, you need to get you some of that sunscreen spray," whispered Harry.

"Yes Harry," she said dryly. "And what I need is for Hanover to apply it,"

By this time Rhonda had packed up and said her goodbyes to everybody. I walked her over to the van. She said, "So it looks like I'll see you at the next event, which should just be in a couple of days." Her eyes motioned over to Natalie. "And good luck with that. I think you have a tiger by the tail there."

Around five that afternoon the party broke up and I helped Harry and Hanover breakdown the pavilion and put back the chairs. I came up to grab the last folding table and almost ran into Kathleen.

"Whoooh, sorry about that. I didn't see you there."

Kathleen didn't waste any time getting to the point. "Carlton, we need to talk."

"Okay, we can talk here."

"No, there still might be people around," she said as she looked furtively around. "Can you meet me by the pool at midnight? Is that too late?"

"No, I don't think so. What do you need to talk about?"

"Why was Natalie asking me all those questions? No, we can't talk about it here. Meet me out by the pool at midnight tonight and I'll tell you. I know it sounds a little melodramatic, but I don't feel safe talking here. There is something I need to know about."

"Okay, I'll be there."

Kathleen nodded and walked quickly back into the house.

I stood there for a couple of minutes trying to figure out what she needed to know. I was still mulling it around when I got back up to the top floor. Natalie had already showered and changed. She looked like something out of the 70s with a tie-dye shirt, cutoff jeans, and flip-flops. She had her hair pulled back into a ponytail and was sitting on the couch sipping champagne.

"What took you so long? I've been waiting here for hours."

"It's been fifteen minutes," I countered.

"Well it seems like hours. What is on the agenda for this evening?"

"I was thinking we could head over to Steamers. I heard they have great seafood."

"That sounds fine to me, cupcake."

"Don't call me cupcake."

"What is wrong with cupcake?"

"It's a food, not a name."

"It's an endearing name," she purred.

"No."

"Well, I have to come up with some little pet name for you. Everybody has one."

"I don't. I don't think we need one, you can just call me by my name."

"But it would be so much more fun to have a pet name, my little Swedish delight." She looked at me hopefully.

"I'm not Swedish."

"What are you?" she asked curiously.

"I'm Czechoslovakian, or I was before the maps got all screwed up. I guess now I would be considered half Czech and half Slovakian."

"My little half-Czech-half-Slovakian delight," she said contemplatively. "No, that doesn't roll off the tongue at all." She sighed. "Okay, I will keep looking, but I'm sure we can find one we will both love."

"I doubt it."

"You wait and see, my little stud muffin."

"Good grief." I grimaced.

CHO
———Ξ———

Chapter 9

I WAS FINALLY ABLE to load Natalie in the car and we headed over to Steamers. I headed down the Beach Road towards Kitty Hawk. Steamers is located in Southern Shores right where the road bends to head for the bridge. It is located in a strip mall, so it's easy to miss. We got there right before the dinner crowd and were able to get seated on the upper level.

The waiter came up to get our drink order. He turned to Natalie.

"I think I'll have either a Sweet Mama, Sex on the Beach, or a Pain Killer. Which do you sell the most of here?"

"Ma'am, I've only been here a week. I don't think I've heard of any of those. Most people just order a beer."

Natalie turned to me. "CR, which of those would you prefer?"

I gave her a big grin.

"Oh never mind, I know what you want," she said in an exasperated tone. "I'll have the Sweet Mama. Make sure they use a half cup pineapple juice, a quarter cup seltzer, one shot sweet and sour mix, and one good shot of tequila. Got it?"

The poor waiter was scribbling all this down. I could just tell he was dreading the actual dinner order. He turned to me.

"I'll have a vodka and tonic, extra lime. Gray Goose for the vodka. Do you have any diet tonic water?"

"Ah, no sir. Just regular tonic water."

Still not sure why everyone hasn't caught on to the diet tonic water craze like I have. "Very well." I sighed acting like it was practically the end of the world. "I'll have it in a tall glass and make sure the tonic water is fizzy. There's nothing I hate more than flat tonic." Might as well educate the lad up front.

We sat and perused the menu until the drink order came. We sipped our drinks and mine was quite good, nice and fizzy with three limes.

Natalie took a sip and nodded her head. "Yes, this is exactly what I needed after a grueling day."

"You sat on the beach most of the day," I pointed out.

"I know, but the men were so needy. They just couldn't get enough of me."

"I'm sure they wanted a lot more of you," I said sarcastically. "How ever did you tear yourself away from all that attention?"

She said with a mischievous smile, "I told them you were a black belt and whispered conspiratorially I thought you might even be wanted in Wyoming for the strange disappearance of a rival for my affection."

"Who was this purported rival?" I said with raised eyebrows.

"Hondo."

"Hondo was your sister's dog."

"CR, never let the truth get in the way of a good story." She grinned.

The waiter came to check up on us, and we both were thirstier than we originally thought so we ordered another round. When the drinks returned this time, I told him we were ready to order.

"I'll have the Pimlico Crab Cake. And with that I'll have a side Caesar salad," said Natalie.

I had eyed that one as well. It was a four-ounce jumbo lump crab cake served with smoked paprika hash, charred broccolini, and smoked jalapeno remoulade.

"Excellent choice. And for you, sir?"

I went straight for the jugular. "I'm going to have a pound of the Wanchese Wild Caught Large White Shrimp. I think I'll also have a side Caesar salad and Hush Puppies. Do you happen to know when the shrimp were caught?"

He looked glad to be able to have a question thrown at him he could answer. "Yes sir, they just came off the boat this afternoon around 2 p.m. They are some really good-looking shrimp."

"Great, how about the Hush Puppies?"

"The Hush Puppies?" asked the waiter, looking confused.

"Yes, when were they caught? I assume you did it quietly," I whispered.

"Geez, CR, have mercy on the guy," Natalie stated, turning to the waiter. "I'm sorry, he was trying to be funny. Usually though, he is more trying than funny."

"Yes, of course. I'll get the order started right away." He turned and hurried away.

"I can't take you anywhere," Natalie said in an exasperated tone.

"Well, I thought it was funny."

"That's the problem, you usually do," Natalie drawled, sadly shaking her head.

For those that don't know, and that would've included me before this week, Wanchese is located well off the beaten path from the typical Outer Banks beach towns, but it has a charm all its own. Wanchese has a long history of being a fishing village and has one of the busiest marinas on the islands. A lot of the locals head over there to stock up on shrimp and fish. The Pimlico Crab Cakes came from Pimlico Sound, which was nestled between the Outer Banks and the mainland. Which was good news because I thought Pimlico was a racetrack up in Baltimore and I didn't want to envision what the crab cakes were going to be made of, if that was the case.

Not willing to have her put a damper on my humor, I asked Natalie, "So, what did you think of everybody today?"

"Well, I thought Rhonda was particularly attractive and seemed to have a good sense of humor and tolerance for pain, since she put up with you."

"I meant the guests at the house, not the caterer," I said dryly.

She looked innocent and batted her eyelashes. "Oh, did you?"

I laughed. "All right, point taken. Now that you have it out of your system, how about the guests?"

She smiled, knowing she had made her point. "As you know, I had lunch with the Crump sisters and Kathleen. We talked about where we came from and what we did."

"Could you be a little bit more specific?"

"Okay, let me think. For example, Kathleen said she grew up in a small town called Mapledale, West Virginia, wherever that is. Her mother still lives in the house she grew up in. The whole town was excited because they just got their first McDonald's. She has a twin sister, although she hadn't heard from her in the last couple of days. She was supposed to be down here but was a no-show. She doesn't like Harry and thinks Hanover is full of himself. She had a fight with him earlier this morning. She didn't say what it was about, but she said she was really steamed over it. She likes the house and said it was like a second home to her. And she didn't like the pork barbecue. Oh, here is an interesting fact, Kathleen and I went to the same university, William & Mary. She was a year ahead of me. Talk about a small world. But I guess we didn't travel in the same circles because we never ran into each other."

"I got the impression she thought you were asking a lot of questions of her?"

"Hmm, maybe I was. Her name sounded familiar, but I am probably getting it confused with someone else."

"Okay, how about the Crump sisters?"

"I'm sure they were both dropped as babies. Talking to them, it was like I had blurred vision or something. I saw two of them but only one person spoke."

"I know, it's rather difficult to concentrate on a conversation when you're bouncing back and forth between them like a ping-pong match," I said.

"Exactly!" Natalie exclaimed. "That is what I was thinking. Let's see, they were kindergarten teachers in Petersburg. They grew up in Petersburg, they went to school together, they went to college together, and they got their first job together in the same school. How freaky is that? They retired and live in Petersburg. They saw an ad Roger had placed in one of the beach magazines that he was looking for some investors in his house and they answered it.

They claim they have always loved the beach. They think something fishy is going on here and it probably has something to do with Harry. Harry was a big topic of discussion. All three of them thought he was too opinionated and chauvinistic. They also thought he was too domineering over Darlene. One of the Crump sisters, I don't know which one, said we should just wait. One day Darlene's going to lose it and, in a year, they're going to find Harry cut up into little pieces in the freezer."

I chuckled. "Go on, she didn't actually say that."

"If I'm lying, I'm dying," Natalie held her hand up in a Girl Scout salute, although I'm not sure she'd ever been a Girl Scout. "And they said it with a little bit too much relish if you ask my opinion. Oh, one other thing, and it's no surprise, the Crump sisters have never been married. Kathleen was but got divorced about five years ago. She kept her married name because it was nicer than her maiden name which was," Natalie paused. "Well, I don't remember, but it began with a D."

"What did you think about Harry?" I queried.

Natalie waved her hand. "Oh, I've seen lots of Harrys in my life. Harry will get away with whatever you let him get away with. He knows how to push people's buttons and he enjoys the drama. The trick is to not fall for it or to use the same philosophy back on him. Some people will never get it, like Hanover for example. Hanover is the type of guy who likes to charge and hit things head on, boom. But with Harry, you have to use finesse."

I told her Harry's philosophy on short women. She sat there with her mouth wide open. "You have got to be kidding me. He doesn't actually believe that garbage, does he?"

"He seemed pretty convincing when he was talking about it." I laughed. "I think he believes there is an element of truth in what he said. He may have exaggerated some parts of it, but essentially, yeah, I think he believes it."

"Well it's a good thing I'm not short then, isn't it?"

I looked smug. "Harry didn't say those traits were exclusive to short women."

For that, I got a rap on my knuckles with her fork.

"Hey," Natalie said with arched eyebrows, "you didn't tell me there were more people coming down and that two people, who were part owners here, had been killed. When were you going to drop that little bit of truth on me?"

"My goodness that was a chatty bunch. I'm not sure how all those pieces fit together, and I didn't want to worry you. Heck, I don't even know if any of this fits together, yet."

"Is that why you didn't want to stay at the house?"

"Well, it is one of the reasons."

"Sure, it was. When I asked Hanover about the other guests, he was a little vague. Although he did say he saw a couple of them on the beach yesterday. He also said one of them was a felon. Did you know that?"

"A felon? No, I didn't know that. What the hell was Roger thinking?"

"He was thinking with his wallet instead of his brain. Which is quite admirable actually since most men don't think with either—they think with their—"

I cut her off. "Did he say who it was?"

"Who what was? Oh, the felon, no, but that's all I've got."

That was good timing because our dinner had just arrived. I dug into my shrimp and Natalie seemed to ooh and ahh over her crab cakes. I was tempted to try to get a bite, but I knew Natalie didn't like to share her food. I'm sure as a child she had written on her report card home that she 'doesn't share her toys with others'.

I politely asked how the crab cakes were and she said they were delicious. "Almost all crab and no filler. And look at the big chunks of crab in here. They practically melt in your mouth."

I leaned over to look closer, but she pulled her plate away.

"Not a chance buddy, stick to your shrimp," she exclaimed.

I sighed and went back to pealing my shrimp. They had been seasoned with Old Bay and steamed to perfection. Bigger than the ones I got at Goombays, the shells just seemed to slip off them. I alternated using cocktail sauce and butter with them, taking a break every now and then to grab a hush puppy. They had brought butter for the hush puppies. It must be a southern thing because I liked my puppies with ketchup, which the waiter promptly brought. We decided to split a cheesecake for dessert, and they brought it on two separate plates. That way I didn't have to get into a fight with Natalie over whose half was bigger. Because in cheesecake, size matters. As the last bite of cheesecake had been consumed, we contemplated having an after-dinner drink but decided we could have a nightcap back at the cottage.

We got out of Steamers, drove around awhile, and walked on the beach before heading back to the cottage. We sat out on the deck awhile before heading back inside. The night had clouded over and there probably would be a shower or two before morning. I told Natalie I had to run an errand over at the house and would be back in a bit.

Natalie looked at her watch. "It's almost midnight. What could you possibly have to do over at the house at this hour of the night?"

I'm going over to the house to meet with Kathleen. No, that was a suicidal answer if I ever heard one. "I forgot something in the bedroom I need for tomorrow morning. It will just take a minute." That sounded a whole lot better. I gave her a quick peck on the cheek and hurried out before she could ask any follow up questions.

I started for the front door but thought better of it. I noticed security cameras on the house across the street earlier and knew if anything went sideways, they'd be looking at them. I went down the inside stairs and out the back door. I crossed the backyard and between a couple of houses to get on to Beach Road. I got to the house a couple of minutes after midnight and noticed for the first time a gate on the side of the house that led to the backyard. I took it. About this time, a light mist had started to fall. There was enough covered area in the back from what I remembered, so I was sure Kathleen wouldn't get wet.

I walked closer to the pool and saw someone was in it. I took a closer look and did a sharp intake of breath. There was a guy, floating. I then saw a crumpled figure on the far side of the swimming pool as well. It looked like Kathleen, or at least someone that was dressed like her. I rushed over to her, ignoring the floating body for the moment and felt her pulse. She had one. She started to stir and groan. I checked the rest of her for stab wounds, gunshots, or blood but there were none. She just had a bump on the side of her head. I breathed a sigh of relief, pulled her underneath the upper deck overhang and leaned her up against the back wall.

I stood up and went over to look at the guy in the pool. He had on blue swimming trunks and sported a Hawaiian beach shirt very similar to mine. I did a double take. As a matter of fact, that shirt looked exactly like one of mine. It was one of the ones I had bought when I got down here. I shook my head and sighed. I walked closer to the pool's edge and saw he had been stabbed in the back. I took a picture of the body with my cell phone and blew it up so I could get a closer look at the knife handle. It looked exactly like one of those used on the buffet table at the cocktail party Wednesday night. The detached part of me wondered if Rhonda realized she was missing a knife.

One didn't have to guess too much to figure out who the body was. Or was that supposed to be 'whose' body it was? Regardless, it appeared Hanover Bennet had taken his last flight and would no longer be able to reach for the stars. I shivered and looked around but nobody else appeared to be there. Kathleen was still unconscious, but I could tell she was slowly starting to come out of it. So, I did what any normal person would do in the same situation. I got the hell out of there.

I backed away from the pool and retraced my steps. I closed the gate behind me using my shirttail to erase any prints. I ran over to Goombays thinking they could give me an alibi, but they had closed at midnight. What bar closes at midnight? I walked quickly back to the house but hesitated to go in and use the elevator because it would register I had used it shortly after midnight, which was presumably when this happened.

I thought furiously for a way out but after a couple of minutes realized I had to bow down to the inevitable. I was screwed. I went in and punched in the code for the top floor. Nothing, again, nothing. It registered that my code was not valid. I banged my fist on the panel and tried it again. It just sat there and blinked at me indicating an invalid code.

I suppose you already caught what I should've realized in the beginning. I didn't have to go back up to the room. I already had an alibi. I smacked the palm of my hand to my forehead, sprinted back to the cottage. I went inside and thought about having a V&T but didn't.

I got ready for bed and that's when I heard the sirens wailing in the distance and getting closer. A little tingle went down my spine when I heard the sirens. I know what you are going to say. I should've stayed and called 911. Let me just put it to you this way—this was the second time a dead body had been dumped on me this week, and quite frankly, I was getting a little paranoid. Okay, a little more paranoid then I usually am. I can see stumbling on one body as a bit out of the ordinary, but two in the span of a couple of days, in the same house, really? Granted, the first body disappeared, but that doesn't take away from the fact it happened. I suppose I could have stuck around just to make sure this body didn't disappear as well, but I was fairly certain it would see the light of day.

I reversed my earlier decision and made a quick vodka gimlet to calm my nerves. I downed it in one gulp. I went into the bedroom, snuggled up next Natalie and fell into a troubled sleep.

———Ξ———

Chapter 10

I WOKE UP THE NEXT morning early. The sun had just started to rise over the horizon. I walked out onto the back deck where I had a limited ocean view, but even so I could tell it was going to be a spectacular day. Or at least I thought it was going to be until I remembered the events from last evening. I replayed everything in my mind, trying to figure out what went wrong and what I had missed. Did the killer mistake Hanover for me? He was wearing one of my shirts and it was dark. I paced up and down on the deck for a while looking at it from different angles until I finally determined I needed to get more information. I needed to know what was going on now and how much everyone knew. I went back inside and figured I could at least get one question resolved.

I called Roger. Roger answered on the fourth ring. In a sleepy voice he said, "Hello? Who dares invade my sleep this early in the morning?"

"Roger, it's me, CR."

With that Roger blinked away his sleep and was immediately awake. "Holy cow, CR, where are you? The police are looking for you."

"Oh, why would the police be looking for me?"

"You're kidding, right? I got a call from the police around 1 a.m. this morning. There was a murder at the house last night. Hanover got stabbed to death. Kathleen is in the hospital with a concussion."

"So, Kathleen stabbed Hanover?"

"That is not what they're saying. But they certainly want to talk to you since you didn't stay at the house last night. The police got everybody up and you were nowhere to be found. They didn't know if you were responsible or something happened to you. Hell, even your car was gone."

"Yes, there was a good reason I didn't stay at the house. When I went back last night to get into the house, I couldn't get in."

"Really? Did you see somebody lurking around?"

"It wasn't that. My key code didn't work."

"Didn't work? Why wouldn't it work?"

"That was the question I was going to ask you. Remember our little conversation where I asked you to change the code after the cocktail party?"

"Oh, that," Roger said guiltily.

"Yes, that. It's funny, yesterday I was able to still use the same code. I didn't really think about it until last night."

"Yes, I kind of forgot to do that so I changed it last night. But I sent you the new code."

I said in a stern voice. "No, you didn't."

"Yes, I did. I sent you an email with it. Hold on, let me pull it up." He rummaged around and I could hear him clicking on his computer keyboard. Then I heard him exclaim, "Oops."

"Oops? What exactly does 'oops' mean, Roger?"

"Yeah, it's still in my outbox. I guess I shut down before it sent. Hold on, I'll send it to you now."

Within a couple of seconds, I heard a ping on my phone. I looked and sure enough it was the email from Roger with the new access code.

"Yes, that really would've been helpful after Natalie and I returned from Steamers last night." Actually, Roger did me a huge favor by not updating the code when he was supposed to. If I had gotten back up to the room at the house, I wouldn't have had any alibi. As it stood now, he gave me the perfect out for not being there.

"Natalie?" Roger said sharply. "What is she doing down there?"

"A free couple of days at the beach…, oceanfront…, with me… Sounds like an easy choice,"

"All except the 'with you' part, I guess so," he said skeptically.

I could then see a light bulb go on over Roger's head.

"Say, if you didn't stay at the house, where did you stay?"

"With Natalie. She rented a cottage nearby. Well in fact, I rented the cottage for her."

"Why didn't she just stay at the house with you?"

"It's complicated," I said. "I think she was going to invite some girlfriends down and I didn't want it to distract me from what I was doing with you." It sounded good. And probably, if Natalie had thought about it ahead of time, she would've done it.

"Good thinking. Well you better get over to the house, call the police or something. I wouldn't be surprised if they had an all-points bulletin out on your little red scooter."

I hadn't thought about that. I was actually surprised they hadn't found me by now since I was so close. But one of the smart things I did, inadvertently, was when I rented the cottage, I put it in the name of Blowhard Technologies and not in my name. It would take a little digging for anyone to figure out and connect it to the fact that I actually lived there. "Okay, I'll go over there right away and clear things up. Roger, any idea who would want to kill Hanover?"

"And then there were seven," Roger said in misery, almost to himself. "No, he seemed like a normal common guy."

"I was afraid you were going to say that. All right, but if you think of anything, give me a call." I hung up the phone. Well, I didn't actually hang up the phone since I was on a cell phone. What exactly do you call it now when you end a call on a cell phone? You don't hang it up, so do you terminate it, kill it, or end it all? They all sound so blood thirsty, so until I hear a better term, I guess I will stick with hanging it up. Sorry, rabbit hole.

Anyway, I went in to roust Natalie from bed. From the time I had gotten up until now, she had taken over the whole bed.

"Natalie, time to wake up, sleeping beauty."

"Go away."

"But the sun is up, the birds are singing, and the ocean is calling."

"Go away."

"Oh, come now, you've had your mandatory eight hours of beauty sleep."

"I only need four, my little Pukka Shell," she said in a sleepy tone.

"Stop that. I am nobody's Pukka Shell," I exclaimed indignantly.

"But I was having the most scrumptious dream." She rolled over, taking half the covers with her.

"Come on, rise and shine. We have a long day ahead of us. Plus, I have some bad news."

Natalie peeked out the window at the crystal blue sky. "What could possibly be bad about a day like today? Didn't you just say the birds were shining, the sun was singing, and the ocean was doing something or other?"

"Err, something like that, yes. I think what Natalie needs is a cup of coffee."

"Do I ever," she groaned. "Two Splenda's and some half-and-half. I will be out in a minute."

I could tell this was 80% poor acting and 20% reality, but I humored her. "Coming right up."

I went into the kitchen and fired up the coffee maker. I don't drink coffee, so I didn't really even think about having all the appropriate supplements needed to brew a good fresh cuppa Joe. I put a Keurig pod of medium roast into the machine and hit the 8-ounce button once the blue light started to flash. I didn't have any Splenda or half-and-half, so I substituted some milk and a Sweet'N Low packet I found in one of the drawers. I didn't think Sweet'N Low had an expiration date, at least I didn't see one on the packet. I put it in the mug and stirred the brew just as Natalie came out.

"Here you go, one fresh cuppa Joe," I said handing her the mug.

She took a cautious sip. "Ugg, this is terrible. What did you put in here, arsenic?"

"No, strychnine, they were all out of arsenic," I quipped.

She took another sip and then dumped the rest of it down the sink. "Whatever it is, I'm sure it'll clean the drain better than anything." She fixed herself another cup of coffee, black. Not her favorite but as they say, any port in a storm.

"You know I went back over to the house last evening, but it was to meet Kathleen. She wanted to talk to me about something in private."

Natalie was still semi-asleep, but that woke her up completely. "Oh, you have a thing for her?"

"No, it was just something she wanted to tell me in private."

She said sarcastically, "I'll bet."

"Anyway," I continued, "when I got to the pool, she had been knocked out and Hanover was floating in the water, dead."

She exclaimed in a startled voice, "What? Why in the world are you telling me this now and I haven't even had my first cup of decent coffee?" She then stood there staring into her coffee mug. "Say CR, you didn't kill him in a jealous rage over me, did you?"

I laughed. Leave it to Natalie to make sure that it was all about her. "Hardly. I am just an innocent bystander in all of this. Let's just leave the fact that I was over there last night between us."

"Okay, have it your way. But it would have been oddly chivalrous if you had ended his life because of your love for me." She added reflecting, "Well, in a bloodthirsty, serial killer, creepy kind of way."

"Thanks. Your faith in me knows no bounds," I said dryly. "Oh, and another thing, I rented this cottage for you, and the reason you don't stay with me over at the house is because you were thinking about inviting some girlfriends down for the week."

"But you're not staying at the house, you're staying here."

"Yes," I said patiently, "but they don't need to know that."

"I think I need to write this down so I can keep track of all the lies," she said grumpily. "And people say I'm difficult to live with."

I ignored that comment, although I did have some thoughts on the subject. "I talked to Roger this morning and he said the police are looking for me, so I need to get over to the house. Besides, they're not lies, they are just omissions of the whole truth."

The look Natalie gave me told me she didn't believe a word of it. "That's okay, I need to write up my review of the smart cover-up. It's a little quirky but it does have potential. Did you know that one of the Crump sisters had a DWI ten years ago? And that one of Harry's neighbors filed a restraining order against him for cutting down some trees that blocked Harry's view of the river."

"How did you find all that out?" I asked curiously.

"I didn't. The smart cover-up did. I need to come up with a catchy phrase for the review like 'eye in the sky'. No, that won't work. Eye on my boobs. No, that just sounds dirty. Anyway, I'll think of something."

I just shook my head and walked away. After I had showered and changed, I came out of the bedroom and gave her a kiss on the cheek as she was watching the local news and the coverage of the murder. I stood there and watched it a minute but didn't get any additional information above what Roger had already told me. I was about to walk away when Natalie flipped to Channel 13. They had just wrapped up their coverage of the murder and switched over to a live shot of

Avalon Peer to highlight that a body had been discovered in the water early that morning by some fishermen. When it rains, it pours, I guess. I held my breath for more details, but they indicated this was a developing story and more information would come as it became available.

I got to the house and parked. As soon as I got out of the car, I was approached by an officer of the law.

"Excuse me sir, are you Mr. Carlton Russell?"

I looked at the officer and a smile crossed my face. "Officer Fenton, we meet again."

Officer Fenton looked a little perplexed for a second until he recognized me. "Are you the gentleman I escorted into the house a couple of days ago? I was wondering why you looked so familiar. I'm sorry I didn't recognize you right away. We meet so many people in this job."

"Not a problem at all," I said smoothly. "I talked to Roger Bennett and he said there was some trouble here last night."

"Yes sir," said Officer Fenton gravely. "There has been a murder. But I'll let the Lieutenant explain all that to you. If you could come with me, sir."

We went into the house and Officer Fenton punched the code in for the top floor. It seemed everybody knew the code for the floor except me. We rode up the elevator in silence, and when we got out there were three other police officers on the floor. I looked swiftly around, and it wasn't hard to tell who was in charge.

Officer Fenton pointed to the police officer. "Lieutenant Candice Gull, sir."

"As in C. Gull?" I asked and arched my eyebrows.

Officer Fenton tried to hide a smile. "I wouldn't mention that to her if I was you, sir. Just Lieutenant Gull would be fine." Officer Fenton introduced me, and the Lieutenant gave me the once over.

"Thank you, Fenton, I'll take it from here." Officer Fenton left and went back down in the elevator. She referred to her notes. "Carlton Russell, I understand from talking to Mr. Bennett that you have this floor in the house."

"Yes, I do," I said candidly and with a smile.

She ignored the smile. "I'd like to ask you a few questions if you don't mind."

"Not at all, I am at your service," I responded graciously.

She ignored my graciousness. "Do you know what happened here last night?"

"Well…" I paused to let her know I was conscientiously thinking it through for the first time. "I had a brief conversation with Roger Bennett this morning and he informed me that Hanover Bennett, no relation to Roger, was murdered. Stabbed I believe he said, and Kathleen Kidd is in the hospital with a concussion. But other than that, I don't know anything. Did it happen here?"

She ignored my question. Apparently, Lieutenant Gull was very single-minded and not easily distracted. "I see. So, walk me through your movements yesterday evening."

"My girlfriend, Christine, and I attended a pool party here in the late morning and most of the afternoon. We came back up here, showered and changed, and then left to go have dinner."

"The information we have" said Lieutenant Gull referring to her notes, "is that your girlfriend's name is Natalie," she concluded, staring at me steadily.

Well, that told me a lot right there. I guess everybody else had already spilled their guts. "Didn't I say Natalie? I'm sorry. Yes, Natalie and I came back up here, showered, changed, and then left to go have dinner."

"And where was that?"

"Steamers up at Southern Shores. It is in a strip—"

"Yes, I know where Steamers is. I've lived here my whole life."

"Oh, so you're a native beach bum," I said pleasantly.

That elicited a sharp glance from her. "And what time did you leave there?"

I guess it was somewhere around 9:30, 9:15. Somewhere in that area, probably closer to 9:30.

"And you came back here?"

"No, we drove around awhile. My girlfriend, Christine—"

"Natalie," she responded impatiently.

I grinned inwardly. "What? Oh yes, Natalie, hadn't been down here recently, so we drove around, walked on the beach, that sort of stuff. We were going to come back here but my code didn't work for the elevator."

"Oh, and who would've provided you the code?"

"Roger. You see, we had a cocktail party here the previous night, and after the cocktail party I asked him to change the elevator code since everyone had access to it."

"Was there a reason for that? Did you feel threatened or insecure?"

"No, it was just my policy to ensure my privacy."

She looked a little skeptical of that answer but forged ahead. "So, the code didn't work," she stated.

"Correct, I found out Roger didn't reset the code after the cocktail party but waited until last evening to reset it."

"What time did he reset it?"

"You'll have to check with him on what the exact time was. But anyway, when we got back here it wouldn't work, so we went over to stay at my girlfriend's cottage."

"And where is that?"

"Oh, it is a couple of blocks over that way." I waved in the general direction of the cottage. She gave me a deadpan stare. I reluctantly gave her the address.

"And what time did you get to the cottage?"

"We left from Steamers about, let's say 9:30, so got here about 11:30 and found out the key code didn't work and got to the cottage at around 11:45-ish."

"Did you see anyone when you got to the house?"

"All creatures were asleep all snug in their beds, while visions of sugarplums danced in their heads," I quoted.

The quote was lost on LG. "And then?"

"We went to the cottage, had drinks on the back porch, and then we went to bed."

"And neither one of you left for the rest of the evening until this morning."

"That is correct. Neither Natalie nor I descended from the cottage decks to wander in the night," I said solemnly. Technically that was true. I went down the inside steps.

"Okay, I noticed that you didn't have many clothes here and I don't see any from your girlfriend, Natalie you said her name was."

"She just got down yesterday, and she is staying at the cottage she rented."

"I see, so you are boyfriend and girlfriend, yet you're not staying in the same house together."

"Since you haven't met Natalie..." I started and stopped. "I mean, once you meet Natalie, I think you'll better understand. We are loosely boyfriend and girlfriend. Besides, I seemed to remember her talking about inviting some girlfriends down for the week. And as much fun as that seems, until you've met Natalie's girlfriends, you don't know what kind of fun you're in for."

She frowned and shook her head. "Okay, that'll be enough for the moment, but I'll need to talk to this girlfriend that you seem to have trouble remembering her name. Can you give me her number so she can come over here?"

I ignored the crack. Two can play at that game. "Well, I can go get her," I said helpfully, pulling out my car keys.

"No, I think it'd be better if she came separately."

"Okay," I said reluctantly and gave her Natalie's phone number. I stood there while she dialed the number and talked to Natalie.

Natalie promised to come right over after she'd had a good cup of coffee somewhere. I think that irritated LG a little bit, but she let it go. She hung up the phone and turned to me. "Your girlfriend said that a decent cup of coffee was more important than coming over here," she said incredulously. "She does realize this is a murder investigation, doesn't she?"

Okay, maybe it irritated her more than a little bit. "She actually said that?"

"Words to that effect," she said disgustedly.

"Don't worry, if I know Natalie, she's going to stop by Dunkin' Donuts, get a big coffee and a glazed doughnut, and she should be over here in twenty minutes."

True to form, twenty minutes later Natalie was escorted up by Officer Fenton. He was chuckling at something Natalie said but wiped the smile off his face as soon as he saw LG.

Natalie was carrying a large Dunkin' Donuts coffee cup and a bag of doughnuts. "Hi honey," she said musically. "I got you your favorite chocolate iced doughnut right here in my ditty bag." She handed me the bag and saluted. I guess she knew a ditty bag was a sailor's term for a small bag used to hold personal items. Sometimes Natalie surprises me with her knowledge.

LG just stared at Natalie. Natalie had on a blue and white striped sailor outfit. Even her shoes were blue and white striped. She sported a Dixie Cup as her headgear. For those who do not have a nautical or Navy military background, that is the white cap that Navy enlisted sailors wear.

LG looked from Natalie to me and then back to Natalie again. "Okay, now I get it," she responded flatly.

"What?" Natalie exclaimed as she saw this look from LG and took another big bite of her glazed doughnut.

LG took a deep breath and let it out slowly. "Thank you very much Mr. Russell, if you could wait over there while I talk to Natalie."

I tried to act nonchalant, but I was actually pretty nervous. I had related to Natalie what our story was going to be for last night and this morning, but she still hadn't had her first cup of coffee. I wasn't sure if she had actually heard and understood it all. I nibbled on my doughnut and after a couple of minutes, LG waved me back over.

"It looks like your girlfriend has pretty much the same story as you do, except she couldn't remember the name of the restaurant but said it had something to do with water. She was able to describe in excruciating detail—the crab cakes she had down to a tee. It had to be Steamers. They are the only ones around to make a crab cake like that. And," she sighed, "she was a little fuzzy on when you got back to the cottage after you tried to get in here. She did say after you all got back there and after a drink on the back deck that she, and I quote, 'cuddled up with my snuggle bunny for the rest of the evening,' unquote."

I turned, glared at Natalie, and said in disgust, "Snuggle Bunny? That's what you came up with, Snuggle Bunny?"

She confessed, "yeah, it sounded a whole lot better in my head."

LG was watching this exchange in perplexed silence. Natalie noticed her look and started to explain. "You see, it's like this—"

I held up my hand to stop her. "Don't even go there."

"But—"

"No!" And I gave her a look meant to curdle milk. She pouted and stomped over to look out the window at the ocean.

LG just shook her head.

"So, are there any leads?" I inquired politely.

"Leads?"

"Yes, you know, suspects. Who done it?"

LG gave a quick laugh. "You don't honestly expect me to discuss an ongoing investigation with a suspect, do you?"

"Wait, what? I'm a suspect?"

"Either you or your nutty girlfriend. We also have to consider the rest of the household guests and any known associates of Mr. Bennett. She said wistfully. "But I'm so hoping it is you or your girlfriend."

"Well, I was kind of hoping—"

"Ain't gonna happen, Mr. Russell. I've got your contact information. We are going to follow the evidence wherever it leads us." She looked at her watch. "We're going to be out of here in about thirty minutes, so you can have the place back. The pool area is off-limits. You'll see the crime tape around it. If you want to get to the beach, you're going to have to go on the outside of the house around the fence." And with that she dismissed me and walked over to a couple of officers to discuss what I can only conclude was police business and not for the faint of heart or an average civilian.

I went over and put my arm around Natalie, and she put her head on my shoulder. "Poor Hanover," she said quietly. "I was just getting to start to like him.

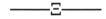

Chapter 11

I WENT BACK OVER to LG and asked if we could leave. She nodded her head and said to stay local. "I don't want to have to go hunting you down if I have any more questions," she said sternly.

"Okay, how long do you think you're going to be here?"

LG answered impatiently, "I told you another thirty minutes here but probably a couple of hours on the property."

I nodded, gathered up Natalie, and left.

"I'm going to go back to the cottage," said Natalie. "I'm a little behind in my work."

"I'm going to go over to the hospital and check on Kathleen. I'm curious to see what her story is," I countered.

We gave each other a hug and waved goodbye to Officer Fenton on our way out. Natalie turned to the right and I turned to the left.

I got to the hospital and went into the emergency room. I asked the receptionist about Kathleen. The receptionist indicated she was resting and was in room 2301. "Just follow the red stripe on the floor and it should get you there."

I did and it did. I knocked on her door and gently opened it. She was resting in a bed with a bandage around her head. She was hooked up to some IVs and a heart monitor was beeping rhythmically in the background. "Kathleen, I just checked in to see how you were."

Kathleen's eyes fluttered and then opened. She turned her head towards me, and I heard her gasp. "Oh my God!" She almost screamed. "You're alive?" she said incredulously. The heart monitor started to beep faster.

I thought that was a little bit of an odd response. "Yes, I'm very much alive," I responded, smiling pleasantly. "I assume no one has talked to you yet about what happened."

"Well...oh my head," she groaned. "I remember I came out to meet you and I saw someone floating in the pool. I started to walk towards him and that's all I remember. I thought it was you!"

"No, it was Hanover," I responded gently.

"Oh no. What happened?"

The police are still trying to figure that out. They're swarming all over the house."

Just then a nurse came through the door. "What are you doing in here?" she said gruffly.

"I'm just visiting a friend."

"No one's allowed in here. Didn't you see the sign?" she asked accusingly.

"Sign, what sign?" In times like these, I have found it is better to play dumb.

She opened the door to reveal a big red and white sign plastered on the door. It read: No Visitors. Police Orders. "You need to leave," she said, pointing to the hallway.

I raised my hands in resignation. "Okay, I'm going. Nice seeing you, Kathleen. I hope you feel better, and I'll talk to you soon."

She smiled wanly and waved.

I was then summarily escorted out of the room. I was so consumed with my own thoughts as I started to walk back to the car that I nearly ran into two people who were hurrying down the hall. I looked up and as luck would have it, one was LG. She did a double take. "Mr. Russell? What are you doing here?"

"I just came over to check on Kathleen, wanted to make sure she was okay."

LG scowled. "You aren't by chance trying to interfere in an official police investigation, are you?"

"No, certainly not. No one told me I couldn't come over here and check on her."

"I suppose that big sign on the door to her room didn't give you a hint?" she said in an exasperated tone. She closed her eyes and took a deep breath. "Well I'm telling you. So if you will just exit the premises, it would be greatly appreciated. I'm sure Officer Thorton will be glad to see you out. She nodded her head at Officer Thorton, and darned if he didn't escort me all the way to the parking lot.

"Say, Officer Thorton, is Lieutenant Gull always so grumpy?"

He smiled. "Murder has a tendency to do that to the Lieutenant. Have a good day, sir."

I thought that over as I drove back to the cottage. When I got there, Natalie had set up a table in the driveway and had some contraption on top of it. She was reading through the instruction manuals as I pulled into the driveway and parked.

I got out and went over to her. "Natalie, what are you doing?"

"I'm reviewing this droid." She had to repeat herself a second time because a single engine plane had flown directly over us at about 300 feet on its way to landing at the airport nearby.

"I see. You do know it's a drone, not a droid. And what do you expect to do with it?"

"I'm testing it out. It's supposed to have a real high-resolution camera and stay in the air for like 45 minutes."

"And you're going to test that here?" I responded, astonished.

"Well of course, silly. What do you think I'm setting all this up for?"

Just then the Red Baron, as it is locally known, flew over. It was a red biplane, and they'll give you a ride around the Outer Banks at fifteen bucks a pop. I watched it circle in the sky as it headed out to the ocean and then back again. "Did you read the part in the instructions about where you have to have the drone operator certified?"

"No, I thought they did that at the factory."

"No, not the drone. The operator. I think you've got to do that with the FAA."

"Oh." She looked a little crestfallen. "Well, let me find the instructions for that. I'm sure I can get that. Maybe I can test drive it later today."

"Probably not, because you see those little planes flying overhead?" I pointed at the Red Baron which by now was only a speck in the sky.

"Sure, that's why I thought it'd be a great idea to try it out here."

"But most pilots tend to frown on having drones flying indiscriminately around in the same space while they're flying around. As a matter fact, I believe the technologies baked into all these little drones is such that if it senses it is in a 'no-fly zone' it won't even work."

"Really? They did mention in here something about a Geospatial Environment Technology (GEO) feature. Whatever that is. Well, I charged the batteries and stuff last night, so let me just see what happens."

"Natalie," I said nervously, "I don't think that's a good idea,"

Natalie grabbed the remote and hit the ON button. The drone's propellers spun around, and it lifted off the table about six inches. Natalie clapped her hands. "See, it's working."

"Natalie," I exclaimed as I edged away. "I think it's probably a good idea for you to put the remote down."

"Oh pooh, let's see what this baby can do!" She turned one of the knobs and the drone shot off. I dove for cover and the drone missed me by inches. Unfortunately, my car was not as nimble. It hit my windshield and shattered it. "Oops!" she exclaimed, dropping the remote.

I got up, dusted myself off and checked for broken bones. Feeling none, I just closed my eyes and shook my head. I guess it could've been worse. She could've actually gotten the drone to go straight up and hit a plane. I went over and looked at the damage. The drone had done a header into my windshield and was halfway in my front seat. I thought to myself, the insurance guys are never going to believe this. I took out my cell phone and took pictures.

"Well, looks like I'm going to have to cross that one off my list. It was probably defective," exclaimed Natalie as she quickly packed up all the instruction books, boxes and remote and hurried into the cottage.

I stood there dumbfounded. I mumbled to myself, "Don't worry Natalie, I'm okay. My car windshield? No, don't give it a second thought. That one was getting old, so it probably needed to be replaced anyway. How am I going to get around? No problem, I'll just hitchhike." I took a deep breath and tried to think of some Zen spiritual calming routine that would keep someone from being pissed off but came up empty. I finally just took a deep breath and concluded Natalie was just being Natalie.

———❏———

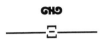

Chapter 12

WHEN I CAME BACK inside, Natalie was on her computer typing away. She looked up. "Oh, I forgot to ask," she said in a concerned voice, "was Kathleen okay?"

All thought to the drone incident was gone from her mind. Sometimes I wished I could live in Natalie's world—a world without care or consequences, full of butterflies and unicorns. I was going to ask her exactly what that world looked like but instead I said, "Yes, she seemed fairly alert when I talked to her. It looks like the worst that happened to her was a concussion. I wasn't able to talk to her much, I got kicked out."

"Oh?"

"Yes, apparently the police don't like you questioning witnesses before they do. Go figure." I shrugged and went and got on my laptop and tried to put the most recent events out of my mind.

We both worked like busy little bees for the next hour or so. I decided it wasn't worth the hassle to go through the insurance company. I did a quick Google search and found a mobile windshield repair company nearby. I called them and they indicated it would take two days to get the windshield in since they didn't have much demand for a 1990 Toyota Camry. I told him that was fine and to text me when they were on their way.

I looked outside and knew we couldn't spend our day sequestered in front of our computers. I picked up the phone, called Goombays, ordered a couple of fish and chips, and then went to the freezer and got out the jug of margaritas I had made the day before. It's sloshed around in the jug like a slushy. I made this batch with bourbon (that I had stolen from the house) instead of tequila (which I had also stolen from the house). It gave it a little bit nuttier and sweeter flavor, so I cut down on the simple sugar and triple sec. I went downstairs to the ground level and found a cooler. I grabbed some ice and put it in large baggies. I put the ice in the cooler along with the modified margaritas. I shut down my computer and told Natalie that we're going to head to the beach.

She nodded as she finished typing. "Sounds like a great idea! I just finished my blog on the smart cover-up."

"What did you finally decide to name it?"

She smirked. "I named it Undercover Cover-up."

"Good one," I said, smiling. "I can't wait to read the write up on the drone.

Natalie pursed her lips and frowned. "I think I'm going to skip that one. I think it was a little bit more technical than I really wanted to go. I'll just ship the drone back to the distributor."

"Do you mean the pieces of the drone?"

"Ha ha, Mister Funnyman," Natalie said. "It wasn't my fault, it was defective."

"Ah huh." I was going to add that the only thing defective was the drone operator but held my tongue.

"Anyway, let's go to the beach," Natalie said cheerfully, closing her laptop.

"I'm way ahead of you. I'm ready to go. I've got the cooler stocked with margaritas. I ordered fish and chips from Goombays. I figured we could drive over in your car," I said, pointedly emphasizing the word 'your'. "We can pick up the fish and chips, park at the house and go to the beach from there. That way we can use their umbrellas and chairs and we won't have to lug them around.

"Great idea. All right, give me a second to get on my bathing suit." A second for Natalie is about fifteen or twenty minutes for the rest of us mere mortals. After thirty minutes she came back out in a pure white one-piece bathing suit with a plunging neckline. And I say plunging, like down to her cute belly button.

"It took you thirty minutes to get into that? You know, we could see how long it takes for you to get out of it. I'll bet it is less than thirty minutes," I said enviously.

She twirled around in a circle. "That's what I like to hear, a man on a mission. You may get your chance at that once we get back. But for right now, I'm hungry for some fish and chips and some sun."

We headed on out. I stared forlornly at my injured mode of transportation as we pulled out of the driveway. Since Natalie drove, I ran into Goombays and got the take-out order.

We got to the house and then I remembered the whole pool area had been roped off. Fortunately, someone had thought about it ahead of time and had taken umbrellas and chairs and set them outside the fence. We grabbed an umbrella and a couple of chairs and went down to the beach. I set up the umbrella, took out the glasses and poured a couple of margaritas on the rocks. We laid out our picnic lunch on top of the cooler. We just finished up the fish and chips and had started on our second margarita when we spied Harry and Darlene making their way down to the beach lugging a cooler, which I guessed contained wine.

Harry set up his umbrella next to ours. "Fancy meeting you here," said Harry. "Glad to see you're alive and kicking? We weren't too sure early this morning. Darlene was betting that you'd been kidnapped by international terrorists and were being held for ransom.

"I was not," declared Darlene. "I said he probably stayed over with his girlfriend."

"Well I know that's what I would be doing if I were him. Sex is always better at the beach, am I right?" Harry said and winked at me.

Natalie was about to fire off a retort when I interjected. "It's pretty tragic what happened to Hanover last night, isn't it?"

Darlene stated, "It sure is, he seemed like a nice enough sort of guy. He didn't deserve what happened to him."

"Yes," added Harry, "Darlene and I were sitting out on the back deck having wine all evening. Hanover came out for a drink, but he didn't stay long."

"Oh, did you all see something?"

Darlene added, "All evening for Harry means until nine o'clock. That's when he goes to bed."

"Oh," I responded, sounding a little disappointed. "I was hoping you might be able to shed some light on why it happened."

"I don't know," piped in Harry. "But that's three down and six to go."

"Harry!" Darlene said. "That's not a very nice thing to say. A man has just been killed. Honestly, I don't understand how you can think about it like that. I think you really need to see a therapist."

"I'm just saying, our ownership shares go up. If this keeps up, you and I'll be half owners of this place in no time at all. That is of course, unless we get bumped off as well."

"Yes, wouldn't that be tragic," I responded speculatively.

"Oh, don't get me wrong," said Harry. "I'm not gonna go out and kill everybody for it, but I'm certainly not gonna mourn over it either."

I had brought extra glasses, so we shared our margaritas with Harry and Darlene. Harry held up the glass and peered at it. "These margaritas got a strange looking color. Are you sure they're okay?"

"They are bourbon margaritas. My own special brew."

"Bourbon margaritas? I've never had one before," said Harry suspiciously.

"Oh, these are delicious," exclaimed Darlene. "We've got to get the recipe. The weekend after we get back, we are going to have my sister and brother-in-law over for a barbecue and these would be just perfect."

Harry sipped the margarita cautiously and nodded his approval. "Yes sir, it's kind of funny how Kathleen got in the middle of that last night."

"Why do you say that?"

"I didn't think she and Hanover got along anymore. I was surprised to learn that they were both down at the pool at that hour. Probably just getting a booty call. I guess that Hanover wanted more than Kathleen was willing to give up. They will probably just list it as self-defense or death by sexual misadventure."

"Anymore?"

"Eh?"

"You said they didn't get along anymore?"

"Yeah, when we first started coming down here, they were a hot item. And then it just stopped. I guess he's the one that broke it off because she was so mad that she could chew up nails and spit out barbed wire. But I guess they learned to overcome it and at least pretended to get along."

"I was at the hospital earlier this morning and checked in on her. Looks like she's going to be okay, but she did complain about a headache."

"We tried to get some more information out of that Lieutenant woman, but she wasn't in a giving mood. Lieutenant Candice Gull. You get the irony there, don't you?" Harry laughed.

"Yes, I got it."

"Her parents must have had a wicked sense of humor," continued Harry. "Unfortunately, none of that got transferred down to her. She had a hard time believing I was with Darlene all night."

Natalie and I had another margarita. Both Harry and Darlene were quick to offer their empty glasses for a refill as well. "Yes indeed," said Harry, "sure would be nice to own a place like this." He sighed.

"I heard there's a provision in the contract that allows you to buy people out."

"Oh?" said Harry without interest as he rummaged around in the white canvas bag they brought down with them. He pulled out a pair of headphones.

"I even heard that everyone got letters offering to buy them out," I baited.

Harry just stretched and yawned. "It's probably just a vicious rumor or one of those mail scams."

"You haven't by chance gotten a letter like that, have you?" I asked innocently.

Harry gave me a blank stare. "No, can't say that I have."

"Harry?" said Darlene.

Harry gave Darlene a look and she stopped what she was going to say. "But that's an interesting thought," continued Harry. "Let's see, he said innocently, "now with three gone, if someone could buy up the other six shares... Yes, that would make for an interesting discussion with Roger, wouldn't it?"

"Well, it's all just idle speculation, I guess."

"Certainly it is, don't give it another thought," Harry responded as he leaned back in his chair and put on his headphones.

Darlene said, "he likes to listen to audiobooks. He won't pick up a book but audiobooks, he's got hundreds of them that he's read. It's the only time I get a little peace and quiet is when he's listening to them."

Natalie coaxed me into applying her Maui Babe Browning Lotion and I didn't mind a bit. It was very distracting but in a good way. I applied the oil over every inch of her body, and Harry made sure I didn't miss any spots.

Just as I was finishing, my phone rang. I grabbed a towel and wiped the oil off my hands. I wandered away from the group so they couldn't overhear the conversation.

It was Roger. "How's it going down there?"

"It goes. Everyone has talked to the police and they're off doing police stuff. I went to visit Kathleen in the hospital this morning. It looks like she'll recover."

He breathed a sigh of relief. "At least that's good to hear."

"Oh, what is the not so good to hear? Has something happened?"

"Yes," Roger said bitterly. "I just got a notice from two of the people that are supposed to be down here this next week that they're not coming?"

"Did they give a reason?"

"Yes, they did. They said that they had sold their interest to another investor."

"I thought you said you all couldn't sell it to outside people."

"They can't, they sold it to someone who was already an investor."

"Oh. Did they say who?"

"No, they said they're being held under a nondisclosure agreement and if it was determined they had told someone, they wouldn't get the money and would have to pay some type of penalty."

"That sounds a little bit like a scare tactic to me. I do know that it's almost impossible to enforce a nondisclosure agreement."

"Enforceable be damned!" responded Roger strongly. "It's not whether it's enforceable or not. It is whether they believe it to be enforceable."

"Is there anything you can do about it?"

"Not a damn thing," he said bitterly.

"Where exactly did you find these lawyers that made up this agreement?

"Craigslist," he said gloomily.

"Oh, that's not good."

"No kidding. Have the police made any headway?" he said, shifting gears.

"Not that I know of, but it's still the early stages. It hasn't even been 24 hours. I'm sure there'll be a lot of action tomorrow once they get back any forensics or autopsy information. Although I don't think the autopsy will go that quick."

"Did they find a murder weapon?"

"It was on the tip of my tongue to say, yes it was a steak knife from the cocktail party, but I stopped myself. I wasn't supposed to know that. "I don't know, the police haven't confided in me."

"No," he grumbled, "they haven't confided in me either. All right, I guess I was just calling you to vent a little bit. Call me when you get some news." And he hung up.

The phone rang again, and I picked it up. Before I could get out my standard greeting, the voice at the other end of the phone said, "Hickory or oak?"

"What?"

"Hickory or oak? We are having a debate on this end. Carlos says oak is the way to go, but I'm thinking hickory. You don't see hickory in a lot of homes every day. It will add a little class to the house."

"E, is that you?"

"Well that's a dumb question. Who else would be calling you asking about hickory or oak?"

Good point. "Oak or hickory what?"

"Floors and cabinets."

"Do you even have the foundation and the walls up yet?"

"Boy, you really don't know anything about homebuilding, do you? Naw, we're working on that next week. We need to order the other stuff because if it's hickory, it's gonna take a couple of weeks because it's not as easy to find as you would think. If it's oak, we can go down to the local Walmart and pick that stuff up. But I'm pretty sure you want hickory, not oak, right?"

My mind was in a fog. What type of flooring for my townhouse was probably the furthest thing from my mind. I said off the top of my head, "Actually, I'd like koa wood, but I guess if you can't find that then hickory will do." And with that, I hung up the phone. Let her chew on that for a while. Little did I know that it doesn't pay to kid with E. It was an expensive lesson I was only going to learn later. If I thought hickory was expensive, koa was over the moon.

By this time, I had walked down to the surf and had my feet in the sand as the waves crashed over them. I was just starting to relax when the phone rang again. What was this, Grand Central Station? I answered the phone. "What?" I barked.

"CR, is that you?"

Oh crap, it was Denise. "I am so sorry I answered the phone like that. It's been one of those days. How are you doing? I've missed you."

"I miss you too. This is almost the first time I've been able to catch my breath."

"Yes, I saw you on Good Morning America or Wake Up Washington or whatever the name of it was."

"Man, don't get me started. I was ambushed on that one."

"How are you making out?"

"It's a long story best told over a glass of wine. I did want to find some time to come see you, but I understand you're out of town."

"Yes, I'm down in the Outer Banks, actually in Kill Devil Hills working on a project."

"Are you going to be down there long?"

"Probably the next week or so, why?"

"Well, I'm driving down to South Carolina to visit my sister and maybe…" She left the rest of the sentence hanging.

I picked up on it right away. "I think it would be delightful if you could stop by." Did I say that out loud? What the hell was I thinking? Natalie was staying at the cottage. I've got a murderer running around over at the house. And I really didn't want to rent a second cottage.

"That sounds unbelievable," she said excitedly. "Let me text you my schedule."

"When do you think you'll be down?" I responded weakly.

"It's not going to be for four or five days. But maybe we can spend a day or two together."

"That sounds wonderful."

"I can't wait. I'll be thinking about you." And she blew me a kiss over the phone.

"Got it and back at ya."

She hung up and I went back up to my lounge chair and stretched out.

"My goodness," exclaimed Harry, "for someone that's on vacation, you certainly get a lot of phone calls."

I ignored him, closed my eyes, and thought about what the heck I was going to do.

———☰———

Chapter 13

I WOKE UP THE NEXT morning to the smell of burning bacon. I rolled over but found Natalie had already gotten up. I sat up, rubbed the sleep out of my eyes, and strolled into the kitchen. It was a little smoky and the bacon was making aggrieved popping sounds on the cast-iron pan. I cracked open a couple of windows and opened the door. Natalie was standing at the island with a bowl in her hand beating the contents vigorously. I noticed on the island there was a box of King Arthur Flour Cloud 9 Pancake Mix. The table had been set with a placemat, knives, forks and two glasses of milk. I went over to rescue the bacon before it was crisp beyond recognition and turned the pan on low.

"So, what are we up to this morning?" I asked.

"I'm fixing breakfast."

"Yes, I can see that. Is there a special occasion? Is it the first anniversary of our first date? The first time we kissed under the stars in the springtime?"

"No, I just felt that you could use a little special attention."

"Ah huh, and what are you up to?"

"Nothing. I even fixed you a Diet Coke, which I know you love. Why don't you enjoy it out on the front deck while I get the rest of the meal prepared?"

"Okay," I said skeptically. I took the proffered Diet Coke and went out to the front deck and enjoyed the early morning sunshine. It was nice to be alone and listen to the ocean waves in the background, but I didn't have long to enjoy the solitude. About five minutes later a police car rolled up. I didn't have to get out of my chair because the police cruiser didn't roll up in front of our cottage, however it did to the neighbors across the street. An officer got out and knocked on their door and then after a brief conversation, disappeared inside. After about five minutes the officer came out, got into his cruiser and drove away.

I breathed a sigh of relief. Although if I had held it for another thirty seconds, I wouldn't have had to do that because another police cruiser pulled up in front of the cottage and LG stepped out. She walked up the driveway and glanced at my car. She stopped to survey the damage. She then looked up at the cottage and saw me and looked back at the car and shook her head. And I'm not sure if she shook her head all the time or just when she was around me.

She came up the front steps and I greeted her. "Lieutenant Gull, what a pleasant surprise on this wonderful Sunday morning. I hope you get overtime for all the hours you're putting in, and I want you to know that we all greatly appreciate it."

True to form, she ignored my greeting. "What happened to your car?"

Well, I proceeded to tell her with full orchestration and three-part harmony the story of the drone and Natalie. I thought that it would at least get a chuckle out of her, and I did slightly see the corners of her mouth turn up but that was about it.

"I see," she said with a deadpan expression on her face. "I have a couple more questions for you."

"Okay, fire away. By the way, have you had breakfast? If not, Natalie's making some bacon and pancakes."

"No, I've already eaten."

"Okay, but I'm sure I'm—" I was cut off from completing that thought by the smoke detectors going off inside. I remember the day when smoke detectors just gave a little beeping noise and you stood up on a chair with the newspaper fanning it until the smoke got out of the smoke detector and it turned off. But technology has come a long way since then and these smoke detectors actually talked. And they were yelling 'Fire. Fire. Evacuate the premises. Fire.'

LG's eyebrows rose as I nonchalantly got out of the chair and went over to the door. "Excuse me, I think I am needed inside. It won't be but just a minute." I went in to find

Natalie had turned the burner back up to high and the pancakes were slightly charred and smoking. I rushed over and turned off the stove, moved the cast-iron pan away from the extinguished flame and turned on the exhaust fan. I found a dish cloth and went around fanning the smoke detectors to shut them up. One by one they felt that they had achieved their purpose and quieted. Natalie stood there in an apron with a spatula in her hand looking horrified. "Natalie, Lieutenant Gull awaits outside and wants to ask a couple more questions. Can I trust you not to burn the place down until I get back?"

Natalie's eyes started to tear up. "Certainly... Yes, I was just trying to... I think the stove's defective."

I gave her a hug, a tender kiss on the cheek, and another hug. "I know and I appreciate it." I looked into her eyes. "It's the thought that counts. But don't touch anything until I get back, okay?"

She nodded and I went back out onto the front deck, crisis averted for the moment.

"Let me guess, Natalie was fixing breakfast?"

"Yes, but the stove is defective."

"Oh? How defective?"

I pointed to my car and said sarcastically, "about as defective as that drone over there.

LG looked over to the car and then back at me. "Anyway, I just wanted to double check your story. You said you left Steamers, wandered around a bit, and went to the house but couldn't get in. Then you came back over here." LG was nothing but business.

"That's correct."

"And you didn't leave here after that?"

"Correct."

"You know it's funny, when you were over at the house, why didn't you knock on some of the other doors to get them to let you in? That's what I would have done."

I had already anticipated that question. "I didn't want to disturb and wake them up. It was late."

"I see." I could tell she wasn't satisfied with that answer. She tried another tack. "We had an interesting discussion with Kathleen."

"Was she able to identify the murderer?" I asked.

"No, but she was absolutely positive you were the one in the pool instead of Hanover until you came barging into her room yesterday."

"I got that much out of her when she asked me why I was still alive." I said dryly.

She continued, "She also said she had an appointment with you at midnight by the pool."

I knew this was coming. She telegraphed it from a mile away. I had thought through a couple of different answers, but I figured the simplest would probably be the best. Acting surprised I said. "Oh my gosh, you're right. I completely forgot all about that. Natalie and I were having such a wonderful time and of course, once Natalie starts 'cuddling with her snuggle bunny'"—and yes, I used air quotes—"all thoughts of time and space cease to exist." I smiled dreamily.

LG looked like she just swallowed a bug. "That's your story?"

"It's the truth." Well, it was close to the truth.

"Why do I get the impression that's not the whole truth? I guess you were pretty lucky to have"—she used air quotes—"forgotten the meeting.'"

"Honest, Lieutenant Gull." I held up my hand in the Boy Scout salute. Yes, I've actually been a Boy Scout. Yes, I also had to look up the Boy Scout salute recently because I forgot it. Anyway, "I'm an innocent bystander in all this." Now it was my turn to ask a question. "I noticed an officer was across the street earlier. Was there a problem over there?" I asked innocently.

"I think you know perfectly well why he was over there."

"Well it never hurts to ask," I said grinning. Going a little bit further out on the limb I asked, "Did they find any fingerprints on the murder weapon?"

"What murder weapon?"

Now it was my turn to act exasperated. "I think you know perfectly well what murder weapon. The one found at the scene, of course."

"How do you know the murder weapon was found at the scene?"

I smiled enigmatically. "It's a small town."

"That was the other reason I came over here," she said, gritting her teeth. "Tomorrow morning, I need you and Natalie to come down to the station and get fingerprinted. I've already asked the rest of the guests to do so and they have agreed."

"Certainly, any particular time?"

"Will 10 a.m. work for you?"

"We wouldn't miss it for the world."

With that, she about faced, walked down the steps, glanced again at my car, got back in her squad car, and left.

I went back inside and gave Natalie another hug and then threw out the charred pancakes. I added a little bit more pancake mix to the remaining batter, added some milk to that, and a little splash of vanilla. I mixed it all up and turned the stove back on low. I added butter to the cast-iron and then poured the hotcake batter on top of that. I watched it closely because cast-iron is a little tricky and you had to find just the right temperature to correctly cook it. After the third pancake I was able to get it right and we ended up with about half a dozen decent pancakes.

We ate breakfast, and I told Natalie again how much I appreciated her making breakfast. It was really sweet of her. While we were eating, I filled her in on LGs meeting with me.

"CR, when do you think these murders are going to be wrapped up?"

"I don't know. It looks like they're just getting started."

"How long am I going to have to be down here?"

"Don't you like it down here?" I responded, looking wounded.

Natalie smiled. "Don't get me wrong, I love being down here with you, but I was just wondering."

"It could be a couple of days or it could be months depending on the evidence they find. I would think they wouldn't be able to hold us down here for that long, probably just another couple of days."

She looked a little relieved and I didn't press her to explain why.

We spent the rest of the morning going through some thrift shops and the outlet malls down in Nags Head. We headed south on the highway and passed Jeanette's Pier. We crossed over the bridge to Maneo and took a sharp right on Sailfish Drive. We ended up at the Blue Water Grill and Raw Bar. They are a family-owned restaurant, and the place had a feel reminiscent of a coastal boathouse with lots of wood and windows overlooking the water.

We got seated by a bank of windows that overlooked the boats coming and going from the harbor. We started out with a couple of oyster shooters which included a mix of vodka, Bloody Mary mix, cucumber purée, lemon-honey horseradish, and an Old Bay rim. The daily specials were posted on a blackboard written with multicolored chalk. One special was half-off bottle of wine, so I ordered a bottle of Grgich Hills. Natalie ordered the Baja fish tacos, which were crispy fried mahi-mahi topped with cabbage, queso fresco, citrus sour cream, and pink pickled onions. It was served with

Spanish rice and beans. And while I eyed the Carolina Bison Burger, I ended up ordering the Fried Oysters served with coleslaw and hand cut fries and a blue water remoulade. They were a little crunchy on the outside but real full of oyster flavor on the inside. We took our time, sipping wine and watching the boats. We contemplated dessert but neither one of us had any hunger left to do it justice.

After a while, we returned back to the cottage. It was another beautiful day in the Outer Banks. The sun was shining and there was a light breeze out of the east and a couple of clouds floated around overhead. The planes were out with big banners trailing behind them trolling up and down the beach. We went back over to the house and hung out at the beach the rest of the afternoon. We didn't see anybody else, which was nice because that gave us the false impression, we were alone in the world and all was right with it. That's not to say there weren't other people on the beach, but we didn't know any of them.

That evening we went over to the Jolly Roger and had dinner. The Jolly Roger is just a short drive down Beach Road. I had a Taco Salad and Natalie had a Cobb Salad. I think we were probably both feeling a little guilty about our overindulgence and the rich food we had been eating the last day or so.

We got back to the cottage and lounged on the back deck having some Mai Tais the rest of the evening.

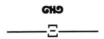

Chapter 14

THE NEXT MORNING, I made sure I got up first and announced that we were going to go to Bob's Grill for breakfast. Their motto there was 'Eat and get the hell out'. The Goombay crowd had already warned me about Bob's. 'Eat and get the hell out' developed during popular and crowded lunchtimes as founder Bob McCoy would move through the crowds at his Kill Devil Hills grill urging lollygagging locals to get a move on so he could seat waiting customers. In addition, the portions were humongous. But I didn't tell Natalie because I wanted her to experience it firsthand. We ordered iced tea and when that came, Natalie hemmed and hawed over whether to get the McCoy's Crab Meat and Cheese Omelette or the Country Fried Steak. She finally settled on the Country Fried Steak smothered with sausage gravy, two eggs, hash browns, and a biscuit. I ordered a side egg over medium.

Natalie raised her eyebrows. "That's it? The breakfast boy is only going to get an egg? You do realize I don't share?"

I smiled. A short time later, Natalie's meal arrived. It covered half the table. Natalie just stared at it helplessly. The Country Fried Steak took up half the plate while the heaping portion of hash browns covered the other half. A second plate held the eggs and biscuit. A small plate was placed in front of me with the egg on it. "Still committing not to share?" I questioned smugly.

"What the heck. Is this a joke?" I held up my hand and waved for her to look around. She did so and found the other plates were summarily stacked with food. "Wow. Okay, let's see how hungry I am."

I had to give it to her. She made a gallant try. But halfway through everything she gave up. "Okay, you win. You can take it from here," she said as she shoved the plates over to me.

I laughed gleefully. "My Natalie finally learns to share. I'll mark this down on my calendar and maybe we can celebrate it annually." I pulled out my cell phone. "Should we call your mother?"

Natalie groaned. "Stop it, I'm too full to protest."

Even with only a single egg in front of me, I couldn't finish all of Natalie's leftovers. The check finally came and as the waitress slapped it down, she said pleasantly, "Thank you for coming, now finish eating and get the hell out." She concluded and waltzed off to tend to another table.

"Did she say what I think she just said?" whispered Natalie, wide-eyed.

"Natalie, it was on the sign out front. Big bold letters."

"Oh, right. Now I remember."

After that, we headed over to the police station. We got there right before 10 a.m., went in and told them we were there to get fingerprinted. They did the honors and we left. No LG and no other guests were there. It seemed like much ado about nothing and probably everybody else thought the same thing until later.

That afternoon, we all went out and sat on the beach. Harry, Darlene, Kathleen and the Crump sisters joined us. If we planned it better, we probably would've set up the pavilion, but as it stood, we had three different umbrellas and chairs. Everyone asked Kathleen if she was okay. She downplayed it and said it was good to be back home.

The Crump sisters were huddled underneath an umbrella as were Harry and I, but Darlene, Natalie and Kathleen seemed like they wanted to worship the Sun God and sat out on chaise lounges.

It was a quiet lazy day, but then we heard sirens in the distance. I don't think any of us thought really anything of it until LG and two officers came traipsing over the sand toward us.

"Mr. Harry Patterson," said LG, directing her attention to Harry.

Harry didn't hear her because he had his headphones on. Darlene nudged Harry. That startled Harry and he took off his headphones. "Darlene, you know not to disturb me when I'm listening to my audiobooks. I was just getting to the most interesting part. It was the part towards the end where they were going to unveil who the murderer was."

"Mr. Harry Patterson," repeated LG.

Harry looked a little startled, looked around and saw LG standing there. "Why Lieutenant Gull, and to what do we owe the honor of this visit?"

"If you can please stand up, sir."

"Why on earth would I do that?"

"Sir, you're going to have to come with us. I'm hereby placing you under arrest on suspicion of the murder of Hanover Bennett."

We all were shocked.

"What the devil are you talking about?" exclaimed Harry. "I already told you I was in bed asleep." He started to put his headphones on again.

"Officer Schultz, could you please escort Mr. Patterson to the squad car."

Officer Schultz walked towards Harry and stood over him.

"Well I'll be damned," said Harry as he stood up. "Has the world gone crazy or what? All right, I'll come with you, but don't expect to keep me. I haven't killed anybody."

Officer Schultz attempted to guide him by putting a hand on his shoulder, but Harry just shrugged it off. "Don't touch me. I know how to walk to a squad car."

All the while Darlene was clucking, "Harry? Harry, what are they doing? Harry, I don't understand what's going on."

I got up to reassure her it would be okay. "I'm sure they just want to ask him more questions." I could certainly figure out why they were taking Harry though. Obviously, his fingerprints showed up on the knife. That only led me to believe the murderer had taken that knife from the cocktail party and used it to stab Hanover. It was pretty clever. But then my other inner voice kicked in. Maybe Harry is the one that did it and since his fingerprints were on the knife, no one would believe the criminal could be that dumb. Either way it was a red-hot mess.

Everybody scattered after LG left with Harry. Darlene went running back to call her son, Harry Junior, to find out what to do. I thought to myself if all they had on Harry was that fingerprinted knife, it was going to be a hard sell. Harry was a good talker, and he would be quick to point out anybody had access to that knife with his fingerprints on it. He would also argue he was in bed the whole night. It wouldn't take a great lawyer to get the charges dropped.

But now the hunt would be on trying to figure out who had taken the knife and when. Also, in the back of my mind was still the fact that maybe Hanover wasn't even the intended target. I don't think LG had caught the significance of him wearing a shirt very similar to mine, or if she had, she wasn't letting on. Maybe this was some gambit on her part to put the real murderer into a false sense of security. I sat looking at the ocean and ran through all the different possible reasons in my head. When I finally looked around, I was alone. I guess Natalie, Kathleen, and the Crump sisters had lost their vim and vigor for the ocean and decided to go back inside.

Chapter 15

I PUT AWAY THE CHAIRS and went back upstairs. Natalie was sleeping on the couch. I decided to go over to Publix and get something for dinner. We had been eating out way too much.

I mulled through my mental rolodex of dinner recipes and decided on Beef Stroganoff. I got some good round steak, two pounds of mushrooms, and some flat noodles. I also picked up some asparagus and the rest of the ingredients. If you're interested in the recipe, it's in the back of the book. I turned on the news as I was chopping onions, mushrooms, and prepping the beef. Hanover's murder apparently had piqued the beach crowd and was being widely reported again. They now said they had a suspect in custody. I just rolled my eyes. There was an update on the body found at Avalon. Apparently, a group of revelers had been partying down there and had gotten into a drunken stupor. One of them evidently wandered into the waves and couldn't find his way out. I was oddly disappointed it wasn't Kathleen's sister.

I had finished putting everything together and added a splash or two of red wine. It's not in the recipe, but who could argue with adding a little vino. The stroganoff was bubbling merrily on the stove as I washed the asparagus. Most people cut the ends off, but I have found that by snapping them toward the end, it snaps right where the more tender part of the asparagus begins. I wet a paper towel, wrapped the asparagus in it, and laid them out in the microwave. I filled up a pot with water for the noodles, added a little salt, and put the pot on the stove but didn't turn it on yet since sleeping beauty hadn't woken up. I fixed myself a V&T and went out on the deck.

I was sitting in a chair relaxing and thinking of a happier time—one without dead bodies and complicated lives. I thought that after this little fiasco, I was going to travel someplace, anyplace. My phone rang as I sat there daydreaming about where to go.

"Hello this is Carlton Russell. How may I help you?"

"Mr. Russell, it's Rhonda."

"Rhonda, how are you doing? Haven't heard from you in days, but I'm sure you've been kept busy."

She laughed. "Yes, and not necessarily in a good way. The police have been keeping me hopping, and some of my loyal customers are starting to raise their eyebrows."

"Well, it'll all blow over. I assume they put bamboo underneath your fingernails and shone a bright light in your eyes to get you to confess."

"Confess to what?"

"Stealing that knife and stabbing poor Hanover."

"Oh no," Rhonda said in a horrified voice. "They were just interrogating me on how I store and transport my cutlery. Who had access to it? What are my cleanup methods? What exactly did I do after the cocktail party last time? Did I take an inventory of everything beforehand and afterwards? Stuff like that."

"And did you?"

"Did I what? Oh, take inventory? Of course. There was a knife and a fork missing but that's not unusual. Everyone likes to take home a little souvenir from time to time. I mean it's not something I would report to the police, for Pete's sake."

"I'm sure Lieutenant Gull thought differently."

"She certainly gave me a look to make me think so. And I'm sure when I reported it, they would take it as the number one crime of the century and put it in their online police report. Knife and fork stolen at the Bennett party last night, news at eleven." The last part she said in a deep broadcaster voice.

I laughed. "Well, they do now," I observed.

"Yes," she responded in a perplexed voice. "I honestly don't know how it went missing. Oh, I know how, but anybody could've taken it at any time during the evening. It's not like we had them under lock and key."

"I'm sure everything will work out in the end."

"I guess so," she said wistfully and sighed. "Right, but that wasn't the reason for my call. We've got another cocktail party going on tomorrow night at your place and on your floor."

"Oh, I guess I do remember something about that."

"It looks like there's only two new ones coming in, Hastings Meadow and Love Tablue."

Hastings, Love, and Hanover—whatever happened to normal names like Bob, Jeff, Mike, Sally, and Jane? I shelved that conversation with myself for a later date. "Are we going to have the pleasure of the two other local people that were there before?"

"Noella Weathers and Buddy Yardley? No, they both had other pressing engagements."

"I'll bet they did," I responded sarcastically. "Nobody wants to be at a cocktail party where a day later a member of said cocktail party has been murdered. It's not good for your political reputation. Although, I would've thought a newspaper woman like Noella would jump at the chance to be there."

"Noella? She does society and a lot of the fluff pieces. No, this time you get Brendan McCall. He's a real jackass, pardon my French, and I'm sure he just relishes a good murder. He does all the investigative reporting stuff. We are also going to be blessed to have Meredith Bottlemore of the

Corolla Wild Horse Fund. They have taken on the task to protect, conserve, and responsibly manage the herd of wild Colonial Spanish Mustangs roaming freely up there."

"Why didn't the murder scare her off?"

"She can smell money and publicity a mile away. She's quite passionate about her horses."

"Sounds interesting. So, what are we going to have at this shindig?"

"Oh, so now it's a shindig? I thought it was a soirée."

"No, the last one was a soirée, so this one's definitely a shindig for sure."

"Whatever you say." I could almost see her rolling her eyes at me. "We're going to be having a lot of finger food. Nothing that requires sharp objects. We're having crab puffs, mini crab cakes, oyster shooters, and fish sliders."

"Doesn't some of that require some type of utensil?"

"Yes, I've been told I can have sporks?" she said in an amused way.

"Well there's a blast from the past."

"Hey, I didn't make up the rules. Anyway, we will be there at seven o'clock and it kicks off at 7:30. Roger gave me your code, so I'll be able to get right up."

Yeah, I thought to myself, how sweet of Roger to be doling out my security code like candy at Halloween. "Okay, I'll make sure I'm not in the way."

"Oh, and I forgot to mention, Lieutenant Gull will also be there. I mean, it wouldn't be a party without her."

"Are we talking about the same Lieutenant Gull?"

"Oh, Candace isn't that bad. I went to school with her. She was always a bit serious and a bit of a tomboy at the same time. I'll bet you didn't know she was the kicker for our high school football team. They came in second at State her senior year. We grew apart a little bit when we both went to college, but she was right there when my husband died."

"I'm so sorry, how did he die?"

"Training accident. He was a pilot in the army. His chopper went down in bad weather. Candace stayed with me for the week after it happened making sure I didn't fall apart. It was touch and go there for a while." She sighed. "That was a horrible year. My stepfather died around the same time as well."

"Wow, when did all this happen?"

"It's been about four years now. I'm getting over it and moving on," she responded bravely.

I said dryly, "I've been telling that to my therapist for years now and he still doesn't believe me."

She laughed. "You're funny. And I can completely understand why you need a therapist."

"Hey, cheap shot!" I exclaimed and paused. "All kidding aside Rhonda, I am sorry for your losses."

"Thank you for that. Okay, I gotta run. And if you want to get in good with Candace, be nice to the horses. She loves them as well." And with that she hung up.

When I got back inside, Natalie was fixing a salad. "Who's that on the phone?"

"Rhonda, she's letting me know we have another cocktail party up here tomorrow."

"Oh goody, the last one went off so well."

"Now, now, sarcasm doesn't become you," I scolded her. "Remember, we've committed to being a kinder, gentler people this year."

"Sure, and that is working for you how?"

"You were supposed to have had a refreshing nap, not one that made you fresh. If you please, can you throw those noodles in the boiling water?" While she did that, I added the sour cream to the stroganoff and turned the burner off. Once the noodles were done, I started the microwave for two minutes to cook the asparagus.

The wine I paired with this meal was a Courtney Benham Cabernet Sauvignon from the Stags Leap district. It had firm tannins supporting a rich palate of cassis, brambleberry, and black cherry, while the nose carried notes of pepper and raspberry. There were touches of mint and oak in the finish. Now I had never laid eyes on a brambleberry and I think cassis refers to black currants, but all in all, it was a good wine. I tasted some of those elements but not all of them. Maybe the V&T had deadened my taste buds. Natalie seemed to appreciate it though, and we polished off the whole bottle by the end of the meal. We finished the dinner with some apple pie and ice cream. I had to admit I had been snacking on the apple pie I had gotten from Morris' so there was only enough for one helping each. That was probably a good thing since my meal to dessert ratio had gotten a little out of whack lately tending to the dessert side.

We cleaned up after the meal and put the leftovers in some Tupperware to take back to the cottage.

Natalie looked around after we had finished. "Can't we stay here tonight?" she said as she snuggled up to me. "The ocean breeze is lovely through the windows, the sound of the surf, and just us...together...alone."

"Yes, but you forgot to mention the murderer that is probably lurking on the premises," I said reluctantly. That splashed a little bit of cold water on the mood.

She slowly detached herself from me. "Okay, let's go before I talk you into it. I certainly don't want to not wake up tomorrow morning because someone turned the gas on while we were sleeping. The way things are going, that's probably what would happen."

We left and went back to the cottage.

———☐———

Chapter 16

TUESDAY DAWNED AND I got up early. I reheated some stroganoff and had that for breakfast. It was even better the second day. I was just putting the dishes in the dishwasher when my phone rang. I looked at the caller ID and scrunched up my nose. It was Mo. I kind of figured he'd be calling sooner or later. As you remember, Mo was my CEO at Blowhard Technologies. I was sure by now they'd seen the credit card charge for the cottage, and of course I'd done absolutely nothing to earn it over the last couple of days. I picked up the phone nonchalantly. "Carlton Russell, how may I help you?

"CR, this is Mo."

"Oh, hey Mo. How are you doing?"

"How am I doing? The real question is how are you doing? You see, I get this report every Monday on any unusual expenses within the company, and guess whose name popped up?"

I said hopefully. "Nathaniel Gibson in IT? I keep telling you he's buying way too many desktop computers for everybody."

"No, it wasn't Nathaniel, it was you."

"Oh, huh. I wonder what that's all about."

"As if you didn't know," he responded acidly. "You do know I'm not going to be able to approve these charges on your credit card."

"Well Mo, I was hoping to earn that money by meeting with some partners down here."

"We don't have any partners in North Carolina, CR."

"That's the point. The North Carolina coast can be a great place to explore using wind technology."

"And how much headway have you made in that area this last week?"

Well, he got me there. "Not much, but hope springs eternal."

"CR, unless I see some tangible results, you're going to be on the hook for that charge."

"So, you're open to the idea?"

"I am skeptically, reluctantly, open to the idea with very low expectations of your success."

"Gosh, that sounds almost like a yes," I responded dryly.

He laughed. "What's the real reason you're down there? I thought you had enough excitement up in your own neck of the woods with that O'Hara murder. Don't tell me you found your way into another one?"

"What could possibly make you think of that?"

"I do watch the news. Especially when someone like you pops up on the radar."

"I'm sure whatever it is will be cleared up in the next day or so."

"It'd better be."

"Say, I don't suppose Blowhard Technologies would like to donate to the Corolla Wild Horse Fund. It's tax deductible."

"Hardly," he replied. "At least not without good reason. What would the corporate interest be in doing that?

I was going to say it would get me in good with LG and maybe I could get more information on the case, but what I really said was, "Being philanthropic?"

Mo laughed. "CR, you do realize we're a for-profit company."

"It was just a thought."

"Keep me informed on what great partnerships you're building down there, and if it's significant enough, I may consider approving this."

"Okay Mo, see you later." I hung up the phone feeling a little depressed. I mean, true, I did own the company and I guess I could have trumped him, but one of the reasons I have Mo is exactly for this reason. I needed Mo to take care of the company while I tried to figure out how to take care of myself. This was getting to be an expensive vacation.

Natalie got up shortly after and was almost human after her second cup of coffee. I looked outside and the day didn't seem particularly promising. I looked up to the west to see dark clouds. I suggested we go over to the house and we might possibly get some beach time in before the rains came in. Natalie said she would rather go out shopping, and so we parted with me going to the house and her looking to contribute to the economic well-being of the Outer Banks. When I got over to the house, Officer Fenton was just coming out and heading over to his squad car. I waved to him and asked, "To what do we owe the honor of your company today, Officer?"

"Just clearing up the crime scene and releasing it. I understand Mr. Bennett is having the pool company come over to sanitize it this morning, so it should be fully operational early this afternoon."

"Well that's good news. It means you're closer to catching whoever did this, right?"

"We have a number of leads that we're following up on," said Officer Fenton noncommittally.

"Do any of them include me?"

Officer Fenton smiled. "Anything is possible."

"Any word on when you're going to be releasing Harry?"

"Why would you assume we are going to be releasing him?"

"You mean other than the fact there really isn't any direct evidence to connect him to the crime?"

"Well, that's not my call. Lieutenant Gull will have to determine when Mr. Patterson gets released. We didn't actually arrest him—we only brought him in for questioning."

"But you kept him overnight?"

Officer Fenton shrugged. "We had a lot of questions."

"I see. I understand we're going to be having a little shindig this evening and Lieutenant Gull is going to be in attendance."

"Yes sir, that's my understanding as well."

I continued to ask questions of this font of knowledge hoping to get something, anything out of him. "Yes sir, I'll bet you didn't know we're getting two new guests."

"They are hardly new, sir. They've been down here for the last week."

"Oh, so you've talked to them?"

Officer Fenton hesitated. "We may have had some conversations with them."

"And did you learn anything?"

Officer Fenton looked uncomfortable. "Sure, you always learn something when you talk to people, assuming you talk long enough. Beyond that, there's really nothing I can tell you." He looked at his watch. "I need to be running along. Have a good afternoon and evening, sir." With that, Officer Fenton climbed into a squad car and drove off.

I know Officer Fenton didn't tell me much, but it did get my mind thinking along different lines of inquiry. Those other two guests had been down here this whole week and everybody else in the house were all suspects. How certain was I one of them did it? Maybe one of those two had grand plans and evil thoughts. It'd be interesting to size them up at the party this evening.

I went inside and up to the top floor. It was just how we had left it the evening before, but somehow I got the impression someone had been there. I looked around and nothing was missing. But something was different, I just couldn't put my finger on it. I shrugged. I had brought my computer along, so spent the afternoon researching some potential local partners.

Natalie came by about five o'clock all excited. "Guess what I'm going to be wearing to the party tonight?"

"One can only guess," I responded automatically.

"I'm going to come dressed up as a pirate. I got everything, the bandanna, and I even got a patch to put over my eye."

"Natalie, this is not a costume party. You are not going to be coming as a pirate."

"Yes, I am!"

"No, you are not. I forbid it." I knew that was a mistake the moment it left my mouth.

Her posture went from wounded to defiant. Her eyes flashed. "I'm sorry, what did you say?"

"I said it wouldn't be a good idea," I responded lamely.

"No, you didn't. You said you forbid it. Let me tell you one thing, mister"—heavy emphasis on the word 'mister'—

"nobody tells me what I can and cannot do, especially you!" Heavy emphasis on the word 'you'. And with that, she turned and stormed out of the house.

Oh boy. I blew out a breath I didn't realize I had been holding. I contemplated running after her but thought she needed some time to cool off because nothing I was going to have to say would she be in the mood to hear. I forbid it? Where the hell did that come from?

I went and got a V&T, filled up a glass three quarters full of ice and cut up a lime. I squeezed a slice around the rim of the glass and grabbed the can of diet tonic out of the refrigerator. The bottle of Grey Goose was sitting on the counter so I liberally poured a couple shots into the glass, added the diet tonic, squeezed in two extra lime slices and stirred. The elixir of life accompanied me out to the back deck.

I took a deep breath of the wet soggy air and brought the glass to my lips and froze. My addled brain had finally figured out what was different. What was my Gray Goose bottle doing sitting on the counter with the other liquor? I always keep it in the refrigerator, and I was pretty positive it was there last night before we left. I went back to the kitchen and dumped out the V&T. I took down a clean glass and poured some vodka from the bottle into it. When I held the glass up to the light, it looked a little cloudy. I smelled it and it made my nose wrinkle. I put down the glass and sneezed.

If I was irritated before, now I was down and out mad. That bottle of Grey Goose was only half empty. There has to be a penalty for alcohol abuse, and I'm sure it included being horse whipped, and double it for good vodka. I found a permanent marker in the drawer and put a little black dot at the bottom right-hand corner of the label and put the bottle underneath the sink in the back.

The pantry had another bottle of Grey Goose, and although it wounded me to the core, after the seal on the bottle was broken, I poured out almost half of it down the sink. Well, okay, I took a swig or two of it before I poured just to ensure it was safe to drink. I repeated the steps to make my V&T. I put a little 'x' in the bottom right-hand corner of the label and put the bottle back on the counter.

———⊟———

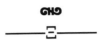

Chapter 17

A LIGHT DRIZZLE had started as I sat on the deck. I watched the drops splatter as I sipped my V&T. When it started to rain harder, I retreated into the house and sat on the couch, trying to figure out what was going on from the tapestry of different clues and events that had happened over the last week.

Everything still seemed out of focus, and after a while I gave up. Sometimes not thinking about something yields more results than actually thinking about it. I was sitting there daydreaming when the elevator pinged. Rhonda and her entourage came out with carts. She looked around and spotted me and waved. I nodded back and as promised, I stayed out of her way as they set up.

Once they got done, it looked like a repeat from the previous cocktail party except plastic sporks had replaced the usual utensils. I smiled at that. But the upside was we probably wouldn't find somebody floating in the pool with a spork sticking out of their back.

I went up to Rhonda when it appeared there was a lull in the action. "Everything okay here?"

"Just great. I think we out did ourselves this time."

"Oh?" I said as I wandered over to the buffet trays.

Rhonda pointed out the crab puffs, mini crab cakes, oyster shooters, and fish sliders. It all looked and smelled fantastic. My stomach started to rumble, reminding me of the fact I hadn't had lunch. I reloaded my V&T and grabbed a couple of each of the buffet items. I was able to polish everything off before everyone started arriving. The crab puffs melted in my mouth, the oyster shooters had a great spicy kick to them, and the fish sliders were crunchy on the outside and moist and tender on the inside.

I put my plate in the sink and wandered over to the elevator. I specifically wanted to be at the elevator door as it opened, and people came out. Was anyone going to be surprised to see me standing upright? Did anyone pay particular attention to me and my V&T?

Everyone started showing up almost at once. Rhonda greeted them all at the elevator and introduced me to Brendon McCall and Meredith Bottlemore. LG arrived, and I almost didn't recognize her in civilian clothes. I never got any reactions from anybody getting out of the elevator. I was hoping for a surprised or scared look on somebody's face, but everybody looked so normal. It was disappointing and frustrating.

"Lieutenant Gull, it is a pleasure to see you again. I hope you enjoy your evening." LG's eyes were darting around taking inventory of who was there. "Can I get you something to drink?" I asked pleasantly.

Her eyes finally settled on me. "Mr. Russell. Certainly, I'll have seltzer water, on the rocks, lemon twist, no straw."

"Would you like anything else added to that?" I asked.

"No."

I could already tell she was going to be the life of the party. While I was over getting her drink, the elevator doors opened, and Harry and Darlene came in. Everybody came over to them asking questions. Needless to say, Harry was in his element and provided everyone great details of the trials and tribulations he went through while being locked up in the pokey. You would have thought the way he told it he had just gotten his death row sentence commuted right before the guillotine fell. LG was just off to the side and watched. I brought her the seltzer water.

"My, my what a pleasant surprise. Did he have a clever lawyer, or did you just see the error of your ways?" I said glibly.

"Neither," LG said sourly and shook her head. "But if that guy so much as jaywalks, I'm going to put him in jail again. Talk about embellishing the truth."

I tried again. "When did Harry get out today?"

"Early this morning." LG looked at me curiously. "Why do you ask?"

I just wanted to know if Harry was the one that poisoned my vodka. That would probably have put a dampener on the party, so I didn't even go there. "Just wondering," I responded airily. "It didn't seem like anybody knew he was here until just now."

"Oh, you noticed that too." She turned and looked at me. "You seem to be taking these matters a little too lightly, Mr. Russell. That is a dangerous habit to get into. I don't suppose you have some information that would help this investigation, do you?"

For a split second, I thought about taking her into my confidence and unloading everything I knew or suspected. But you know what they say about a split second, it doesn't last long. "Who me?" I replied innocently. "I'm just an innocent bystander in all this."

"And yet you are still here. I find that a little odd. A normal person would have cut and run by now."

I was going to offer a witty retort to that comment when the elevator doors opened, and Natalie waltzed in. She had on a black and white bandanna which pulled back her hair and an eyepatch with a treasure chest on it. She was wearing a midnight blue strapless, sleeveless, body contour dress with laces up either side. She also had on a loose-fitting gold chain belt with a short sword strapped to it. I think she was supposed to be a pirate princess and she pulled it off admirably.

Needless to say, all conversation stopped and jaws dropped as she exited the elevator. "Holy Mother of God," whispered LG.

She walked by Harry and reached out with her index finger to lift his jaw back up to close his mouth. Rhonda was delighted. Kathleen looked angry and the Crump sisters visibly reddened. Brandon immediately closed in on her and it looked like he was going to propose marriage to her on the spot. It was exactly the effect she was looking for and she gave me a smug smile from across the room. She whispered something to Brandon, and he went over to the bar and ordered a Grog for her. I'd seen her get that drink before and this was classic Natalie. When she played a part, she really played the part. The Grog was just a prop for her pirate character, although it was actually introduced into the British Royal Navy in the 1700s and not by pirates. But then again, as Natalie says, never let the truth get in the way of a good story. It was concocted by mixing an ounce of lime juice, brown sugar, and dark rum with four ounces of water.

Once the excitement of Natalie's arrival had died down, LG spotted Meredith and motioned her over. Meredith came over and we started talking about the wild horses. I noticed as we talked that LG had positioned herself so she had a full view of the room and could watch everything that was going on. I could tell she was itching to go over to Natalie to see if that short sword was real. I'd say there was about a 50-50 chance it was. After a bit, she excused herself and wandered over to talk with Natalie and Brandon. I was continuing to chat with Meredith about the wild horses when Harry came up.

"Well Carlton, looks like I'm gonna live to fight another day." Harry stated smugly. "I told them it was horse manure to drag me down there in the first place, but they didn't listen. Darlene was finally able to get a lawyer but by the time the lawyer got down there, I didn't need her."

I introduced Harry to Meredith and mentioned she was with the Corolla Wild Horse Fund.

"Yes, I was just mentioning to Carlton about our upcoming event, the Mustang Rock & Roast."

"Oh, that's great," exclaimed Harry. "I always wanted to go to one of those. Now, about the roasting part, I do have one question."

"Certainly, ask me anything."

"Do they taste like chicken or beef?"

Meredith's face reddened. "I'm sure I don't understand your question?"

"When you roast them, do they taste like chicken or beef?"

I was going to interject but then thought, naw. Meredith's hand shot out and slapped Harry across the chops with a resounding smack. The sound was like a cork being released from a champagne bottle.

All eyes turned to Meredith and Harry. Luckily, Rhonda was nearby and had heard the tail end of the conversation. She hurried over to console Meredith and led her away. Meredith was giving her an earful. They were joined by LG.

Harry smiled, ruefully rubbing his cheek. "Apparently, our Meredith doesn't have a sense of humor."

I smothered a smile as Darlene came running over. "Harry, what did you say to that woman? Was it something obscene?" Darlene looked worriedly over to me.

I said philosophically, "Obscene depends on a person's point of view. Although, I think Meredith made her point of view on the subject quite clear." I smiled and asked to be excused. I went over to join the aggrieved. Natalie had noticed something afoot as well and joined me.

"Meredith, I sincerely apologize for the comment Harry made. I am sure he was just kidding and didn't mean it. In order to make amends I'd like to donate $100 to the wild horse fund."

Natalie inquired, "What comment Harry made?" The three women were more than glad to recount the event adding a little bit of embellishment.

After the explanation had been given and everyone had finished glaring at Harry, Meredith spoke. "Mr. Russell, thank you very much. Any contribution to help these horses is always appreciated."

Natalie turned to me. "CR, $100? Are you serious? Those horses need our help and protection," she said sweetly. "I was reading about them online. Come on, my little teddy bear." As she said that, she patted my cheek and wrapped her arm around mine. "I know you can do better than that."

I reddened at the teddy bear comment but was helpless to berate her. LG, Meredith and Rhonda were all looking at me expectantly. I cleared my throat. "Actually, my little Chihuahua," I said, glaring at Natalie, "you are right as you so usually are. Shall we make it $500?"

"Ohh, teddy bear." She pouted and said in a sing-song purr, "My scrumdiddlyumptious teddy—"

"Right, right," I said hurriedly. I was sweating. "What was I thinking? $1,000," I exclaimed as I untangled myself from Natalie. "Let me just go get my checkbook."

I started to turn away when I heard Natalie proclaim, "Oopsie. Oh, honey bear, look what I found in my scabbard?"

I turned back resignedly. "Shall I hazard a guess and say my checkbook?"

"Yeppers!" she said happily as she handed it to me.

"I have a pen," interjected Meredith.

Have you ever felt like you've been in an ambush? You walk confidently into a fight with a sharp knife and are faced with a hundred desperados all carrying machine guns and bazookas. That was exactly how I felt. But I took it like a man. I wrote out the check and handed it to Meredith. Rhonda was grinning foolishly, and I even caught a smile on LG's face. They knew I had been had, but good, and they were loving every minute of it. I indicated I needed a drink after that performance and left the ladies chatting excitedly between them. Apparently, one way to unite some women was to get one over on a humble and well-meaning guy—me being the humble and well-meaning guy in this example.

———☐———

Chapter 18

I WANDERED OVER to the bar, poorer but a lot wiser. I asked for another V&T. The caterer turned to the table with the liquor, came back and said they were out of Grey Goose.

"What are you talking about?" I said in an annoyed voice. "As far as I've noticed, I'm the only one drinking it."

"I don't know what to tell you sir, but the bottle isn't there."

I started thinking to myself. What would someone want with the vodka bottle? Anyone could have taken it, but it would have been noticed, unless…" I glanced around the room and my eyes settled on Rhonda. No, it was a crazy thought. I shook my head and turned back to the caterer thoughtfully. "So this catering business must keep everybody busy."

He agreed. "This year has been particularly busy, I'll give you that."

"I'll bet it keeps you close to home since you got to get all this together at such short notice sometimes."

"You bet. Although it was tough this last month or so, because Rhonda was out of town."

"Oh, vacation?" I asked with a quickening pulse.

"No, we try to take our vacations in the winter when it is slow. She said it was family business."

"I see. Well, it's good to know she is available for these cocktail parties."

"Are you kidding? She had those dates circled on her calendar for months. I know she wouldn't miss them for anything."

I asked for and got a glass of Kendall Jackson Chardonnay. I was mentally kicking myself. How could I have missed it? It was sitting there staring me in the face the whole time. She had the means and the opportunity for everything, but the only thing I was missing was a motive. It couldn't have been personal because she didn't know many of the people, so maybe it was the house. On a hunch, I went out on the deck and called Roger.

He answered on the second ring. "What's up CR, any news?" he said anxiously.

"No, nothing yet, but soon, I hope. Roger, how did you get the house?"

"I bought it," he exclaimed in a surprised voice.

I said in an exasperated tone, "I kind of figured that. Who did you buy it from?"

"The city."

"Okay, keep going."

"Well, it was an auction. They had a couple of houses they put up for auction that I guess they repossessed through bankruptcy or nonpayment of property taxes or something. As I remember, there were three properties for sale that day. This one, and two others that were further along the beach. One was up in Corolla and the other down in Nag's Head.

This was the first one on the auction block, and I bid on it. There was another guy who really wanted it and his name was…" Roger paused, trying to remember. "I forget. It will come to me, but anyway, he didn't get it, I did. I stuck around for the other two and the same guy bid on the second one. He didn't get that one either, but he did get the third one. Preston Dudlow. That was the guy's name. Man, I haven't thought about him in years.

"So, what happened was I took possession of this one and some guy out of New York got the one in Corolla. Preston ended up with the one in Nags Head. It was a tough break for Preston because when they inspected it, he found a bunch of structural problems—probably due to the last hurricane—and ultimately had to tear it down. Since it was so close to the beach, the town wouldn't allow him to rebuild so he ended up with a vacant lot. He lost everything. I think it was like a month or two later he died.

"The guy from New York made out like a bandit though. Last I heard he was renting the place for $10,000 a week. I didn't want to rent mine out like that since it is such wear-and-tear on the house. I just wanted a place to come down, relax and possibly one day retire."

"Thanks Roger. I'll be in touch."

I hung up the phone, reflecting. Rhonda had indicated her father died about four years ago, and that would've put it right around the time Roger bought the house. If she thought Roger had caused her father's death, that could be a pretty good motive.

I was going down the checklist to dot all my I's and cross all my T's when Natalie strolled up. "Hello, my little teddy bear," she purred

"Don't call me teddy bear," I said automatically. I shook myself out of my contemplation and turned to Natalie. "So, are we even now?"

She said coyly, "I don't know what you're talking about."

"You know exactly what I'm talking about. That little show to get me to pony up more money for the wild horse fund."

"Pony up?" She laughed. "You are so funny sometimes. Oh that. Well, you deserved it. You were being a meanie and you know it."

"You're right. I shouldn't have said what I did." I took her hands in mine. "I apologize. Your outfit does look tasteful and stunning."

"Thank you," she smiled "You are forgiven. So, what are you so deep in thought about?"

"I was just thinking about Rhonda." Man, I knew that was the wrong sentence to have come out of my mouth at that point in time. What is it with me and saying the wrong thing? Ugh.

"Oh," she said icily, dropping her hands from mine.

I explained in a hurry. "No, not like that. What I was thinking was her father died a couple of years ago. And her husband died around the same time."

"Yes, I know," she said, thawing out a bit.

"You do?" I said surprised. "How do you know?"

"Girl talk. It's common knowledge."

"Do you remember her father's name?"

"No, it was never mentioned. Her husband was in the army, and his name was Benjamin, Benjamin Quick."

"Okay, thanks," I responded thoughtfully.

"What does Rhonda's history have to do with anything?"

"I'm not sure yet, but I think I've got a good idea."

"Changing topics. Have you met the two new guests, Hastings and Love?"

"No, not yet. I was trying to unravel the mystery of the missing GG bottle."

"CR, sometimes you make no sense whatsoever. Come on, let's mingle."

With that, Natalie led me over to talk to Hastings and Love. We found them in an animated conversation with Kathleen. Kathleen apparently was bringing them up to date on everything that had happened. You could see the looks of concern and horror on their faces.

Hastings and Love were not like I had pictured them. I thought Love would be like a throwback to the 70s and show up in a tie-dye shirt, bead necklace and a black MIA band around her wrist, but she was almost the opposite. She was about as tall as Natalie with red hair. It was cut short on the sides and flat on top. She was dressed in conventional beachwear and didn't have a tan that I could tell. She had freckles on her face and arms.

Hastings on the other hand looked like he belonged on Skid Row. I would've thought with a name like Hastings, he would be a doctor or a lawyer, but no. He wore tattered jeans and docksider shoes with a hole in the toe. His hair was long and scraggly and almost came down to his shoulders. I put them both in their mid-30s.

Hastings' speech was slow deep south, and Love's was definitely New York. Love turned to me. "Mr. Russell, I understand you're down here to figure out who did this horrible thing."

I held up my hand. "No, that's the police's job. Roger just invited me down for the week. I am like you, just an innocent bystander."

Kathleen frowned. "You certainly don't act like an innocent bystander," she exclaimed. "As a matter of fact, you ask a whole lot more questions than an innocent bystander as well."

Hastings jumped in—well, meandered in is probably more accurate. "Well, Mr. Carlton Russell. I'm sure we're happy to have you here. We almost didn't come. Most of my family said I should just bail and give this up as a lost cause. And I told them, I don't give up nothing."

Love added, "Even after we got those letters."

"Oh, you got letters?" I asked cautiously.

Kathleen raised her eyebrows again. "You know perfectly well everyone got letters because you were asking about them the other day."

"Was I?" I smiled. "It must've slipped my mind." I said it more to irritate Kathleen than anything else. Why was she acting so belligerent today? "What did you do with the letters?" I responded to Love.

"I threw mine away," said Hastings. "Ain't nobody gonna make me give up something that's mine."

Love nodded her head vigorously. "That's true, me either."

Switching topics, I asked, "I understand you've already been down here a week. It's a shame you couldn't stay here at the house."

"I had a couple of college buddies that had rented a house down in Manteo, so I've been staying with them," stated Hastings.

"And my grandparents have a little cottage in Southern Shores. It's not much and certainly doesn't have a view like this, but I was still at the beach. I was lucky to have it this last week because my brother, his wife and kids are coming down next week."

"You should've stopped by. I'm sure everyone would've loved to see you down on the beach."

"Well, I came down a couple of days ago, but no one was down there," offered Hastings. "I did stop by one time and talked to Hanover. Love and I were able to connect one evening and we went to Mulligans. I love that place. The steamed crab legs are awesome."

Love blushed slightly, and you could really tell with her complexion. "It wasn't like it was a date or anything," she added hastily. "Anyway, we're staying down on the floor below across from Harry and Darlene. Hastings has the back bedroom and I've got the one in front. At least until tomorrow, and then I'll move down to the first floor because the Crump sisters are leaving."

"Oh, they're not going to stay for the meeting at the end of the week?"

Love shook her head. "No, they're not. Don't ask me why."

"Interesting." Getting curious, I left Natalie to continue to chat with them and I went over to the Crump sisters. "Ladies, good evening. I'm sorry we haven't been able to spend more time together."

"Oh, Mr. Russell. It's been…"

"…an exciting couple of days. As a matter of fact…"

"…it's been a little too exciting for us, so…"

"…we're heading home tomorrow."

"Oh, when will you be back?"

They looked at each other. "We're not…"

"…coming back."

"Really, and why is that?"

"Remember we told you…"

"…about the letters?"

"Yes."

"Well we decided to…"

"…take them up on it. And besides, we found…"

"…this nice little house in Corolla. It's small…"

"…but the living is all on one level."

"Even though we will get paid less…"

"…than we think our share is worth…"

"…it'll be a great down payment on that house."

"We can rent it out some of the months…"

"…to pay for the mortgage."

"Plus, it's got a beautiful view…"

"…of the ocean. It's probably a little bit…"

"…too close to the ocean, but…"

"…by the time the sea levels rise…"

"…we will be long gone."

My neck was starting to hurt from all the bouncing back and forth. "I'm sure Roger's going to be sorry to lose you."

"Oh my, we haven't told him yet…"

"…so please don't say anything."

"We're going to tell him when…"

"…we get back to Petersburg."

"My lips are sealed," I said solemnly.

"And we certainly hope you…"

"…solve this wretched situation here."

"I will certainly try," I said. "I noticed you don't have anything to drink. Would you like me to get you something from the bar?"

"Soda water would be wonderful," they both said, and practically in unison.

"That's great, I'll be right back." I went to the bar replenish my wine and came back with their seltzer water. Once I handed it to them, I was able to tell which was Isadora and which was Theodora. I remembered Isadora was left-handed and Theodora was right-handed.

"We noticed…" said Isadora.

"…you're drinking wine tonight."

"Yes," I said sadly. "They apparently ran out of my vodka."

"Well, that's odd," said Theodora.

"Why is it odd?" I questioned.

"Earlier this evening we saw…" said Isadora.

"…Rhonda carrying the bottle around, and it was…"

"…over half full, or about half full."

"Or maybe they just…"

"...misplaced it."

"Did you notice anything else unusual?" I questioned.

"Well"—they looked at each other—"she is spending..." said Isadora.

"...a lot of the evening talking..."

"...to that policewoman."

"We think they're..."

"...lesbians," whispered Isadora.

I laughed. "I am certain anything is possible. Have a good evening, ladies, and I hope to talk to you before you leave."

I left them and started to wander over to talk to Rhonda and LG, but was intercepted by Brendan. "Mr. Carlton Russell?"

"I must be, and I am," I quoted myself.

"If you got a second, I've got a couple questions for you."

I glanced over at Rhonda and LG, and they were sipping their sparkling water and chatting. "Sure, fire away."

"So, I understand you are down here to solve these murders."

I raised my eyebrows. "Murders, plural?"

He had a quick little grin on his face. "Yes, the two that happened before this week and then this latest one."

"I see, you know about those."

"It didn't take long to make the connection."

"Does Lieutenant Gull know about this?"

"She will tomorrow when it's released and online."

"That's not going to make you very popular with her."

He laughed. "Lieutenant Gull and I have a love-hate relationship. She hates it that I find out information before her, and I love it."

"Well just for the record, the police are here to solve these crimes, not me. I'm just an innocent bystander in all of this."

"That's not what I hear. Weren't you also involved in a murder a week or two ago up in Fairfax?"

I shrugged uncomfortably. "Well, involved is a strong word to use. I believe Detective Smith was the one who solved it up there."

"Now that is interesting," he said. "Because I talked to a Margaret O'Hara and she said you were a big busybody over there and butted in where you shouldn't have. But she did grudgingly say you figured out who murdered her husband."

"My, my, you have been a busy little bee," I said woodenly.

He said pleasantly, "that's what I get paid for."

"Let me just say no comment to what Margaret said, and I'll stand by the fact I'm just an innocent bystander down here. I'm helping out a friend who owns the house to do a market assessment."

Brandon raised his eyebrows. "And that's what you do for a living?"

"I have various talents. Some people consider me a jack of all trades and a master of none," I said jokingly.

"The research I've been able to do shows you started and sold a couple of Internet companies a while back. I haven't been able to figure out exactly how much money you made out of it all, but it was a lot. However, since then I can't find anything. It's like you ceased to exist." He continued warming up to his subject. "Yeah, you've got a townhouse in Virginia and a website that indicates you're an executive consultant."

I was going to mention I had a townhouse in Virginia, past tense, until it was blown up, but I figured that would just add fuel to the fire. "Yes, I do some consulting to make a living. But back to these murders," I said, hoping to change the topic of discussion. "Do you have any idea who did it?"

Brandon looked irritated. "No, I'm just getting started. It's like pulling teeth to get any information out of the police, but I've had a lot of interesting discussions tonight with everybody. Even your girlfriend Natalie."

"Oh?" I said. "And what little tidbits of knowledge did Natalie contribute to your investigation?"

"Well for one, she told me you're practically helpless without her."

"She said that, did she?"

"Uh huh. And she talked a lot about the plight of the wild horses in Corolla, which I've already gotten an earful from Meredith. She talked about her blog, her friends back in Fairfax, the latest fashions, the plight of women wearing high five-inch spike heels, and how it is truly tough to find good sushi. Oh, and most people think she's more photogenic on her left instead of her right side."

"Yeah, I'd say if you keep talking to her, you're going to crack this case wide open,"

He smiled at that. "I don't think she has any information that's going to crack the case wide open, but I could just sit for days and listen to her talk. She should write a book."

I thought it would be more accurate to say that she should be hit by a book and a heavy one. "Yes, she has a mesmerizing effect on people," I said neutrally.

I heard over my shoulder, "Are you two boys talking about me?"

"Yes, my little Chihuahua," I said brightly. "Brandon was telling me about how fascinating you were, and he'd like to have more conversation with you."

"Oh!" she said, clapping her hands. "That sounds wonderful, let me get another glass of champagne and I'll be right with you."

With that, she scooted off over to the bar and Brendan just shook his head. "You know you're going to get me in trouble with my wife."

"Ah," I smirked, "don't worry. I'm sure her spell over you will wear off after a while."

GHG

———☐———

Chapter 19

NATALIE CAME BACK, and I excused myself to go over and talk to Rhonda and LG. "Good evening, ladies. Everything seems to be going off without a hitch. Rhonda, the food is absolutely fantastic again. I think the oyster shooters are my favorite, but the crab puffs are a close second."

"Thank you," she said. "The crab puff recipe has been passed down through my family for years."

I turned to LG. "I've been talking to your buddy Brandon over there," I said smiling sweetly, "and he has said a bunch of interesting stuff. I didn't know you shared so much with the local media,"

"I'm sure he has," she muttered. "That little weasel digs into every hole he can find. He's good, but he's not very forthcoming with information."

"Ha, that's funny. He was saying the same thing about you."

"There's a difference between being a police officer and a reporter."

"Don't be surprised if tomorrow you hear about how he's going to be linking the Hanover murder to the others."

That snapped her to attention. "What others?" she said sharply.

Rhonda piped in, "Oh, he must be talking about Benny and Olaf."

LG glared at Rhonda. "You didn't think this was something worth mentioning to me?"

Rhonda stammered. "W-Well," Rhonda said, pausing to regather her thoughts. "I guess I didn't really think about it. I thought you already knew."

LG pursed her lips. "So, what about these people?"

I proceeded to go through the house contract everyone signed, and Roger's dilemma with full orchestration and three-part harmony that explained how everyone was invested in the property and what had happened to them.

"Jesus Christ. Not that it really changes the focus of what we are investigating here, but people, it makes it a little bit more urgent if we have a serial killer in our midst. Is there anything else you're holding from me?"

I hesitated a little too long. That was a mistake. "All right, you're coming with me." She handed her glass over to Rhonda. "Come on, we're heading downtown to the station." That sounded a little melodramatic since downtown was about five minutes away.

"Seriously?"

"Seriously. This has been a long overdue conversation."

"Let me at least say goodbye to Natalie," I went over and said I had to go downtown with LG but would be back shortly. I hoped. "Do not stay here under any circumstances." She nodded, looking concerned. I followed LG downstairs and out into the night.

We got down to the station, and she put me in what I guess could be considered an interrogation room. She came in and put a device with a microphone near me. "We're going to record this."

"Fine by me." I shrugged, acting like I didn't have a care in the world. I didn't have a care in the world, did I?

"Let's start at the beginning, Mr. Russell."

"My friends call me CR."

"I'm sure that's nice for them, Mr. Russell."

I sighed. Okay, it's going to be one of those. I started at the beginning again with full orchestration and six-part harmony. I went through everything that had happened over the last week. I left out the part where I went back over to the house and found Hanover because she didn't really need that much aggravation. But other than that, I pretty much told the truth. Okay, I also left out the fact Kathleen's sister was dead, I had lent Hanover one of my shirts, and the killer probably thought they were killing me instead of him. Oh, I also neglected to mention the poisoned vodka. So other than that, straight truth. And when I got to the end of the story, she was still boiling mad.

"This information would've been nice to have as it unfolded."

"Well, a lot of what I've learned is just observation and conjecture," I said, crossing my arms. "There's nothing really tangible as evidence in any of it."

"So why are you telling me this now?"

So here we come to the ticklish part and I was hoping my donation to the wild horse fund would get me a little mileage. "Because I need your help."

She looked surprised. "Oh, you need my help, do you?" she said sarcastically.

I decided to turn the other cheek and not respond to it. "Yes, I think someone's trying to kill me."

LG blinked and held her breath, thinking of the least biting comeback to that remark. "I'm not at all surprised someone's trying to kill you. As a matter of fact, I was going through a couple of ways to do that just now."

And there, that was the least biting remark LG could muster? Well, there went my thousand-dollar donation out the window. I forced a grin, "I do sometimes have that effect on people."

"No kidding," she said. "And why in the world do you think someone's trying to kill you?"

"Because of the poison,"

Her eyebrows shot up. "Poison? What poison? There was nothing in your statement about poison."

So, I amended my statement to include the vodka and how I had stashed it underneath the kitchen sink and how I had cleverly gotten another bottle to substitute for it. She looked at me in amazement. "You tampered with evidence? You withheld evidence. I should lock you up right now," she sputtered in anger.

"In my own defense," I said quickly, "I didn't necessarily know someone was, well I didn't know it was tied to this series of events until the bottle went missing tonight."

"What are you talking about?" LG said, clinching her fists. "What bottle went missing tonight?"

"Remember I told you I got a fresh bottle of Gray Goose and dumped half of it out and put the bottle back on the counter so the poisoner wouldn't know I knew. You know it really was offensive to pour out..." I stopped completing that thought when I saw the expression on her face.

"Get on with it," she responded angrily.

. "So later this evening during the cocktail party, it vanished. I was so busy watching everybody to see if there was any reaction to me holding my vodka and tonic that I didn't keep a watch on the actual bottle. Evidently, whoever poisoned it must have realized their plan had gone awry and so they decided to get rid of the evidence. I'm thinking if we figure out who took the bottle, we will not only catch the poisoner but the murderer."

"You think that, huh?"

"Elementary, my dear Watson,"

LG looked down at her watch drumming her fingers on the table. "Come on," she snarled. "We're going back to the party. We should be able to get the tail end of it."

On our way out, she asked Officer Hanley to meet her over there. We got back over to the house and went upstairs. She punched in the code. I thought to myself, is there anyone who doesn't have the code to my floor? It looked like Meredith had already left as well as Love. Everything seemed to be winding down. Everyone was getting their last helping from the buffet and filling up their last drink to take with them downstairs.

Rhonda looked puzzled by our short absence and reappearance. I didn't say anything and went back to Natalie, who was out on the deck. I glanced back inside to see Officer Hanley standing out of the way but in direct line of sight with the kitchen. I could only guess his instructions were to watch the cabinet underneath the sink and make sure nobody took anything out of it, and I'm sure LG was making sure nobody left with a bottle of GG.

After about another half hour, the place was cleared out. Natalie stayed out on the deck, watched the ocean, and talked to her friends on the phone while I went back inside. Rhonda had just approached LG.

"Candice, what's this all about?"

"Ask him!" she said, pointing her finger at me.

I proceeded to tell her about the poisoned vodka, knowing full well she already knew about it, and ended up with the disappearing vodka bottle.

Rhonda frowned and was crewing on the corner of her lip. "I see," she said.

Then I dropped the bombshell.

"As I was talking to the Crump sisters earlier this evening, they said they saw you with the vodka bottle, and you were carrying it around."

"What!" LG said sharply. "You didn't tell me that."

I ignored her outburst. "So, the only question we have to solve is where you put the vodka bottle and why you moved it." I didn't take any pleasure in saying that. I liked Rhonda, but if she was some psycho killer, I didn't like her that much.

"Candice," Rhonda said pleadingly. "You can't believe this?" She turned to me. "How could you say things like that about me? I thought we were friends."

I could tell LG was conflicted. She motioned to Officer Hanley, and he went and got a paper towel and opened the cabinet underneath the sink. He crouched down and reached into the back and pulled out the bottle of vodka.

"I didn't put that there!" squealed Rhonda.

"I know, I did," I confessed. "You see, when you came up here earlier this evening, you left that vodka bottle out on the counter with the other liquor thinking I wouldn't notice. I knew I didn't put it there. And when I looked and smelt it, it smelled foul and looked a little cloudy. So, I knew it had been tampered with. I took that vodka bottle and put it underneath the sink and opened a new Gray Goose bottle and put it back on the counter half full. I didn't want you to know I had caught on to your scheme. When you came up with the rest of your staff, you saw I was sipping my V&T and I wasn't affected. At that point, you must have known something had gone wrong and you decided to get rid of the evidence."

"Candice, I have no idea what he's talking about."

I forged ahead. "The real question, Rhonda, is what did you do with the other vodka bottle?"

The silence lengthened as the import of what I was saying hit her. "You think I...I..." Rhonda gulped as her eyes got wide. "I put it in the freezer to get cold," she concluded.

"You did *what*?" I exploded.

"I knew you didn't like warm vodka from the other night. Even down at the beach you had it chilled. Rhonda pointed to the freezer. "So when I saw it on the counter I put it there."

Officer Hanley walked briskly over to the freezer and opened it. There was my missing vodka bottle. He gingerly put his finger on the bottom of the bottle. "It's cold."

I took a step closer. "Does it have a little 'x' on the bottom right-hand side of the label?"

Officer Hanley looked at the bottle. "It sure does."

I felt like such an idiot. I never even thought of looking in the freezer, but by now Rhonda had started crying. Okay, sobbing would be more accurate. LG was glaring at me, and Officer Hanley stood there with his hands on his hips. I was visibly red in the face. I stammered, "Well it all fits together. You weren't here when those other murders were committed this last month."

Between sobs she said, "I was visiting"—*sob*—"my nephew. He was"—*sob*—"in a car accident in Winsor."

"But your father died after Roger bought the house four years ago."

"My father died four years ago after a long battle with colon cancer."

I gave up. Great, I thought to myself, this just gets better and better.

LG was gritting her teeth and I'm sure took sadistic pleasure in saying, "Officer Hanley, can you please escort Mr. Russell to the station and lock him in a cell overnight. That way we can at least keep an eye on him and make sure he doesn't screw anything else up."

Officer Hanley was grim faced. "Come along with me, Mr. Russell."

I sighed. It was going to be a long night. I went out to tell Natalie the situation. Well, I told her I had been asked to confer with the police downtown and it would probably take all night. I kissed her good night and told her absolutely not to stay at the house and to go back to the cottage. She looked concerned but seemed to take it in stride. I'm sure she would get the whole story from everyone as soon as I left. And if I had to hazard a guess, she would probably agree I deserved at least a night in jail. Quite honestly, I agreed as well. I had jumped the gun and botched the whole thing up.

———☐———

Chapter 20

I SPENT A LONG, lonely night in jail. I thought through every detail I had collected throughout the week trying to understand where the right pattern was. Because there's always a pattern. Sometimes it's not obvious at the beginning, but if you look hard enough, it's there. There was something right at the edge of my consciousness that was itching to come into focus, but I couldn't tease it out. It was something someone said, and I had filed it away to follow up later but didn't. I slept fitfully on the hard cot they placed in the cell and woke up to the sound of a key clanking in the lock. I rubbed the sleep out of my eyes as the door creaked open. After having to listen to a lecture about interfering and impeding a police investigation, I was released. I walked outside to a bright sunny day. I was a free man once again.

I checked my cell phone and OBXToday Online had just released their story by Brendan. I guess I was lucky to get out when I did because when LG read it, she would probably blow a gasket. The story went something like this. Death Stalks the Outer Banks. New England string of unsolved murders are connected to our very own 'Pool Murder'. The police have released the only suspect without charging him with the latest murder. And while the police are baffled, a bloodthirsty killer still lurks among us. An anonymous source tells us even Outer Banks local residents are being accused wrongfully of this murder. Millionaire Roger Bennett has hired a detective to look into the murders. It went on to talk about the other two murders, and while I wasn't mentioned by name, I was sure I would be in the sequel, especially if Brandon was allowed to write it. I shook my head and caught an Uber back to the cottage. Also, calling Roger a millionaire was a bit of a stretch since he probably owed as many millions as he owned.

On my way to the cottage, I got a text from the windshield replacement company to say they would be there at 9:00 a.m. sharp. The text told me to leave my keys on the car's dash and they would replace it. I got to the cottage, left the keys on the dash, and entered the cottage without using my cottage key because Natalie had forgotten to lock up. That woman dances with the angels. The windows were open, and a nice ocean breeze was blowing through the cottage. I looked in the bedroom. Natalie was sprawled out on the bed diagonally and snuggled up with a body pillow. I gently closed the bedroom door so I wouldn't disturb her and went into the kitchen to make some breakfast.

I decided today was going to be a cheese and mushroom omelet day. I found some Bisquick in the pantry and made some biscuits to complement the omelet. I also chopped up a little bit of onion and added some ham. I turned on the coffee maker when I heard Natalie stirring in the other room, knowing it wouldn't be too long before she emerged. The biscuits were coming out of the oven, and I had just flipped the omelet when Natalie emerged.

She gratefully grabbed a cup of coffee I had prepared with two Splenda and some half-and-half. "So how is my almost-convicted felon this morning?" she asked, sipping at her coffee.

"Ha, ha, very funny. I just slightly miscalculated."

"Slightly?" Natalie raised her eyebrows. "Accusing Rhonda of all the world's crimes and murders. What were you thinking?"

"Well, it seemed like a good idea at the time."

"I'm sure you were much safer in that jail cell then you would've been if you'd stayed at the house. They were roasting you slowly over an open fire and were even questioning your manhood. Which I defended, of course."

"Of course," I said dryly.

"But after a while the mood lightened slightly as they all recognized you'd be spending the night in a cold lonely dark jail cell to atone for your sins," Natalie said pleasantly.

"I'm glad my misfortune was able to brighten their evening." I paused a moment. "Honestly Natalie, I thought I had it all figured out. Everything seemed to line up, and then it evaporated right in front of me."

She gazed at me over her cup of coffee and said confidently, "You'll figure it out. You always do."

That made me feel a little bit better. Natalie was always quick to point out the errors of my ways, of which there were many, but she has always been very loyal and believed I could unravel the mysteries of the world if I tried. I shared the omelet with her, and we had a grand breakfast. She put salsa on top of hers, wanting to give it a southwestern flair, and I added butter and honey to my biscuit.

I moped around the house for the next hour or so before Natalie said she was ready to go to the beach. I went in and got my swimming trunks on. When I came out, Natalie was in yet another outfit. This one was a one-piece bathing suit, although to call it that wouldn't give it justice. It was a keyhole crossed-front bathing suit. It had a thong style back, high cut thighs and in the front, it crisscrossed so you could see the middle part of her body. If I thought the guys were watching her with their eyes popping out before, this was definitely going to get them thinking. The whole outfit was tie-dyed, and because the thighs were cut so high, it made it look like her legs extended for a mile. It put the other swimsuits to shame and quite frankly, I was impressed. "Natalie, that suit is absolutely stunning."

"Do you think so?" As she said it, she did a twirl. "I kind of like it myself. And the best part was I got a scrunchy for free when I bought it."

"A scrunchy?"

"You know, something to tie your hair back with, and it matches the swimsuit."

"What will they think of next?" I felt completely underdressed in my blue boxer swim trunks and my Brew Thru T-shirt.

She also brought out matching towels. She opened the first one up and it was screen printed with a picture of her on the towel doing a cheesecake pose. She said, "That one's yours." She opened the second one and it was a picture of me screen printed on the towel. It must have been taken last summer when we were at a pool party or something. I looked a little inebriated and had what I thought was a goofy little grin on my face. "And this one is mine," she said as she hugged it.

I was horrified. "You don't expect me to actually use this towel, do you?"

"Well certainly, silly, that's what I bought them for. And besides, that way we both get to be on top." She laughed. Sometimes her laugh is so infectious, so I started to laugh as well.

"Okay," I sighed. "But don't be surprised if you get a couple of requests for some reprints of my towel of you."

"Nope, it's a one of a kind."

"How in the world did you get them done so quickly?"

"Simpson Jefferies owns a screen-printing shop." She said simply, thinking I, of course, knew who that was, although I didn't. Natalie's universe of friends and acquaintances is vast, while mine could be counted on one hand.

I covered my ignorance by going to the freezer and getting a jug of margaritas. Traditional this time without the substitution of bourbon for tequila. I grabbed a couple of glasses and added them to the cooler with some ice and snacks.

We got outside just as the windshield repair people were pulling away. In the backseat, they left the various pieces and parts of the drone and had cleaned up all the glass on the inside of the car. I reminded myself to give them a great review on Yelp. We piled in the car and headed over to the house. By the time we got down to the beach, we saw Kathleen, Love, and Hastings already camped out there. They were happy to see us, so we set up our umbrella and chairs next to theirs.

Hastings was sporting cut-off jeans and Love was looking enviously at Natalie's swimming outfit. "You've got to tell me where you got that. I would just love to have something like that."

And I'm sure a lot of people would love to see it on Love as well because she had a pretty decent figure. She would've been prettier if she didn't wear glasses, but it did give her a bit of a studious look. She was wearing a green and white vertically striped one piece. I kept my observations to myself though.

"Thanks," laughed Natalie, "this is one of the few I have that I can actually frolic in the waves with without fear of it being swept out with the tide. How is the water temperature today?"

"It's a little chilly at first, but if you stick with it, you get used to it," drawled Hastings.

"Come on my big strong Hunky Monkey. Come play in the waves with me," Natalie said, pulling me toward the ocean. That started a debate with those who were left behind as to whether I looked like a Hunky Monkey or not. How humiliating.

Hastings characterization that the water was a little chilly was like saying Philly fans enjoyed a little beer at ballgames. The water was so 'holy hell' cold it took my breath away. Natalie felt it too, but she wasn't going to give me the satisfaction of letting me know it. We battled the waves for a while, and though I'm not particularly proud about it, I did push her into an oncoming wave once or twice just to get even with her for the Hunky Monkey comment. But in the end, as it always is, she got even with me by jumping on my back just as a big wave crashed into us. I got the brunt of it and staggered out of the waves and back onto the beach, shaking the sand and water off of me. Natalie just laughed gleefully.

We got back to our chairs to dry off. The timing was perfect because Harry and Darlene had just gotten there and were setting up their chairs next to ours. Harry had his back to me as I shook out the towel and started to dry off.

He was taking his time staring at Natalie and sensed the movement behind him. He turned around to face me and had Natalie's picture in front of him, dead center. Harry's eyes widened and he took a step backwards, tripped over his chair and almost did a back flip onto the sand. "Holy crap!" he yelled. Everyone jumped to their feet to help Harry until they realized why he had fallen over his chair. They all burst out laughing. The laughter continued unabated after Natalie showed them her towel.

Even Darlene was laughing. "Harry, you say you always want a pair of 30s. I'll bet for a split second there, you thought you got it."

Harry slowly picked himself up off the sand and set his chair back up. "Carlton, don't ever do that again. You could have cut me down in the prime of my life. Darlene, I need a glass of wine."

Everybody ultimately settled back down and enjoyed the sunshine. After a bit, Love popped up to say, "Hey, I've got a game we can play while we're relaxing. Everybody think of a famous person who has changed the world. But it can't be a president or political figure."

Everyone agreed and thought about it for a while.

"Okay," said Hastings, "I'll start off with my person. It is Gandhi. He influenced everybody across the planet and how to reconcile and work things out without violence."

"I'll do you one better than that," Darlene stated. "Jesus Christ."

"Good grief," groaned Harry.

Darlene gave him a withering glance but continued. "That one man has made his influence known not only across the world but over time. It influences everything a lot of people do today."

"Amen," said Love. "My person is a little bit off the beaten path. I would nominate Hedy Lamarr."

"Now we're talking!" exclaimed Harry. "I think I still have a pinup of her somewhere around. Back in the day, she was a real looker."

"Yes," said Love, "but did you know she was also an inventor. She invented spread-spectrum and frequency-hopping technologies that are the basis for Wi-Fi, code division multiple access, and Bluetooth. Without those, much of what we do today in communication wouldn't be possible."

"Oh, now you're spoiling it for me. There's no way there was that combination of beauty and brains."

"Harry! Don't be a chauvinist," cautioned Darlene.

"Mine is Hitler," Kathleen exclaimed. "And for obvious reasons. He exterminated people and almost conquered the world. I would've taken someone like Napoleon Bonaparte or Genghis Khan because they almost did the same things as well, but Hitler is more recent and memorable."

I piped in. "Mine is Charles Babbage."

There were perplexed looks on a couple of faces.

"He was an English mathematician and invented the mechanical computer, which later laid the foundation for computing into the future. Without him doing that we wouldn't be running around with our iPhones, laptops, and desktops. Think of everything we've been able to do with those in the last 40 years all because of him."

Natalie chimed in. "I think I'm going to vote for Stanislav Petrov." Everyone thought a minute trying to place that name but couldn't. "Petrov was the on-duty officer at the Russian command center for the Nuclear Early Warning System. This was right after the Soviet military had shot down a South Korean airliner, so everyone in the world was on edge. Petrov got reports a missile had been launched from the United States followed up by five more. Petrov was the one who interpreted the data and recognized it had to be a malfunction from the Soviet satellite, and so he didn't launch a counterstrike, thus preventing a large-scale nuclear war. Bet you never heard of him. Boom."

"Yeah, y'all got it wrong," said Harry. "The real famous person that changed the world is Joseph Mortimer Gransville."

"Who's that?" questioned Hastings.

"Why, he's the guy that invented the vibrator."

"What?" squeaked Love.

"Yeah, he's the guy that invented the vibrator. It originally was supposed to relieve muscle tension but look at the way it's taken off since then. What would you women do without it?" Harry said triumphantly.

There was a bit of a stunned silence after that.

"I think I'm going to go into the water," said Love.

"I'll second that," said Darlene.

"I'll join you," said Hastings.

"Me too!" exclaimed Kathleen.

I turned to Harry. "You sure know how to clear a beach. That was the best you could come up with, Joseph Mortimer Granville?"

Harry smirked. "Well, it was certainly better than Hedy Lamarr."

I shook my head and laid back in my chair. I laid there a couple of minutes thinking what an instigator Harry was. And just then, something bubbled up in my mind and came into focus. Something that Harry had said at the first cocktail party. "So, Harry..."

"Yes?" he replied drowsily.

"What was it you noticed at the first cocktail party that was odd?"

"Well for one thing, there weren't enough crab cakes."

"No, I mean when we were talking, you mentioned you noticed something odd."

"Oh that, yes, it reminded me of my eighth grade English teacher."

"What?"

"Yes, Miss Veronica Johnson. She was tall, well everybody was tall when you're an eighth grader, and she had an awesome figure. Really stacked, if you know what I mean. Anyway, we were studying English one day and we were conjugating the verb to be. I wasn't as smart as I am now back in those days, and I was having a little bit of a problem with it. Well, Veronica comes over and leans over my desk to look at the work I've done, and wow! You could see down her blouse all the way to her belly button. And she wasn't wearing a bra." Harry smiled and smacked his lips reminiscing. "Yessiree, I've lived with that vision for the past fifty years."

"And?"

"Well, I remembered the lesson." Harry quoted. "'Are' is the plural form of the verb 'to be'. 'I am' is the first-person form of the verb 'to be'. "'Are' is used for plural subjects whereas 'am' is used for singular subjects. Bet you thought I couldn't remember that."

I was looking confused. "What does this have to do with anything?"

"Oh, it was a comment that was made at the cocktail party, the person said, 'here we are.' There was no 'we'. So, there shouldn't have been an 'are'. The person should've said 'here I am.' Get it?"

"Okay," I said, still looking confused. "Thanks for the update. That was very helpful." Not! I sat back in my chair and tried to replay the first cocktail party when Harry and I were together with other people. It was hopeless, we were together with everyone at one point or another. I was going to ask him specifically who he was talking about, then it finally dawned on me what he was trying to tell me in his own convoluted way. I knew exactly who he was talking about, and also why that comment was so out of place.

———☰———

Chapter 21

I DON'T KNOW WHY I had been putting off making the phone call. I guess I thought I wouldn't need to and that everything will work out. And obviously that wasn't the case, so I dialed the number.

A woman answered on the second ring. "Hello?"

"Hello, this is Captain Sigerson. We haven't met before but I'm calling about your daughter," I adlibbed.

Is anything wrong?" the woman asked anxiously.

"No, no there's nothing, nothing to be alarmed about at all. We're down at the Outer Banks. A bunch of us have been helping out down here with the wild horses, so we want to celebrate their participation."

"Oh?"

"Yes, so I'm calling to see if you can tell me a little bit more about their life. So, when we have a toast, I'll have something I can say."

"Oh, that sounds lovely."

"And after I'm through talking with you, maybe I can talk to their father."

"That won't be possible," she said flatly.

"Oh, is he out of town?"

"No, he's dead."

"I'm so sorry for your loss. No wonder I didn't hear anything about him."

"Yes, it happened a couple of years ago."

"May I ask what happened?"

"It's a long story. My husband, Preston, that's his name, was a bit of a bounder. By that I mean he was never good with money. Don't get me wrong, he was a millionaire—he lost a million and then he gained a million. He was always on for the next get-rich-quick scheme. He fell in love with the Outer Banks and bought a house down there. He had won a lottery, I think in Virginia, which covered some of the cost, and he had some inheritance from his mother who passed away. She left him some land and he sold it to cover the remainder of the down payment.

"Anyway, he went and bought the house. I told him we weren't moving. And it's one thing to buy a house for that much money but then to maintain it and keep it up, pay the taxes, pay the mortgage, electricity, water, and everything else. He just couldn't do it, so finally it went into foreclosure. They sold it at auction. He tried to buy it back. He had made some more money by that time, but what I didn't find out until later was he also took all the money out of our daughter's college fund, drained his 401(k) and mine and put a second mortgage on the house here. He didn't end up with the house he wanted, and the house he ended up winning was no good. He ended up losing everything. It's horrible to say that I found him hanging in the basement one day. We were all devastated. It took years of therapy before we could become somewhat normal again." She gave a large sigh. "But that's water under the bridge. I'm glad everything is finally going well."

"Ma'am, that is such a tragic story. I am so sorry for you."

"Well, that which doesn't kill us makes us stronger," she stated philosophically. "I have only been able to keep this house by working three jobs, and who knows how long that will last."

"Maybe I could talk to her siblings as well?" I wanted to get away from that tragic story. It made my heart ache hearing it.

Sounding confused, she exclaimed, "I only have one child."

"What, no brothers or sisters?"

"No, just one child."

"But that's impossible!" I burst out saying.

I could tell the voice at the other end of the phone broke into a bit of a smile. "Captain Sigerson, I think I would know if I had more than one child."

"Oh no, I didn't mean to imply anything. I was just surprised because I was under the impression there were brothers or sisters."

"No, we were blessed with just one daughter," she sighed sadly.

For the next fifteen minutes I asked innocuous questions about her daughter, but I wasn't really paying attention to the answers. I had gotten everything I needed. And now I knew exactly who the killer was and why. I got off the phone and thought hard. I'd told enough lies and had made a couple of really boneheaded mistakes; LG was going to be hard-pressed to believe me a second time. Especially when I told her I knew who the killer was. I took a deep breath and called the number on the card she had given me.

The ever-efficient LG answered the phone. "Lieutenant Gull."

"Hello, Lieutenant Gull. This is Carlton Russell."

"Yes, Mr. Russell, I am glad you called. It will save me the trouble of tracking you down. We actually needed to talk to you. When can you come by the station?"

"I was somewhat hoping you could come by the house."

"Why would I do that?"

"Well, there's something I need to share with you and it's probably not something you're going to like, but I think it will help the investigation."

"I see. Why don't you just tell me now?"

"I think it would be better if we talked it out in person."

She pondered in silence for a moment. It was so long I actually thought we had been disconnected. "Okay, I'll be over there in about ninety minutes." She hung up the phone.

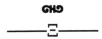

Chapter 22

AFTER ABOUT AN HOUR, Natalie and I headed up to the house.

"I have a project I am going to work on, and I am going to change into my pool swimsuit for later. Maybe we can take a dip in the pool together?" announced Natalie.

"Sure, that sounds like fun," I agreed. "But why do you need a separate swimming pool outfit?"

Natalie rolled her eyes like I had asked the silliest question on the face of the planet. "I am going to don my one-piece electric blue one. Besides, you can't wear a beach swimsuit at the pool. It just isn't done."

"You mean it's done by everybody except Natalie?"

"Exactly," she said gaily and trotted up to our room.

"I went into the pool area to wait for LG. She showed up about thirty minutes later.

"Returning to the scene of the crime, Mr. Russell?" she remarked flatly.

I appreciated the reference, and I couldn't decide whether it was funny or not in this case. "Well there certainly was a crime here, I'll give you that."

"I have some news for you on the vodka," LG stated, watching me.

"Yes?"

"It was poisoned, like you said."

"I knew it!" I exclaimed.

"Yes, it was a very obscure Russian nerve agent that is generally only used by international terrorists."

My mouth gaped open. "What? Really?"

"No, it was rat poison."

I was dumbfounded. LG had actually attempted to make a joke.

I wiped my brow with my forearm. "Wow, I'm glad it was only rat poison. For a minute there I thought you were going to accuse me of being a terrorist or something."

"Don't think it didn't cross my mind."

"Were there any other prints on the bottle?"

"There were yours," she said sarcastically.

"I hardly think I would take the time and effort to commit suicide that way," I replied stiffly.

LG said, switching topics, "What's the real reason we're here Mr. Russell?"

"Like you said at the beginning, we're returning to the scene of the crime. But I'm not sure you have the whole picture."

"Oh?"

"Yes, I may have remembered some additional information which might help you."

LG took a belligerent pose. "I see. Your memory seems to be a bit selective. Maybe you should see a specialist about it."

"In my defense, I didn't really know how it impacted your investigation, and I didn't want to say anything until I was sure. So, here's the deal. I'll tell you everything I know on the condition you hear me out before you arrest me."

She raised her eyebrows. "I'm going to arrest you?"

"Well you're certainly going to want to if the past is any harbinger of the future."

She let out an exasperated sigh. "All right, let's have it."

"The night Hanover died, he was wearing a Hawaiian shirt."

"Yes, we know that. We're the ones that pulled him out of the pool, remember. The question is, how do you know that?"

"Now don't get impatient. I have to tell this my own way."

"Okay, okay, then get on with it,"

"What you may not know is the shirt he had on was actually my shirt."

"How do you know that?" she said quickly.

"Okay, I will tell you but remember you promised not to arrest me until I had finished explaining. You did promise that, right?"

"Okay, fine. I promised," she said ungraciously.

"I actually did come over to the house at midnight the night Hanover died," I admitted. "I saw what he was wearing."

"What? Damn it, Mr. Russell! You are under arrest for falsifying a police report."

"You can break your promise if you want to, but then you won't hear the rest of what I have to say." I said in a wounded voice. "Besides, I didn't falsify it, I just forgot to mention that part,"

I could tell she was really conflicted. It was touch and go there for a minute, but she finally blew out her breath and snarled, "Go on."

"Well, at the cocktail party, we had been kidding Harry about his shirt, you know the one that had the hula dancers on it? No wait, you weren't even there for that. Well anyway, Harry had a Hawaiian shirt with hula dancers on it, and my shirt was a little bit classier but still Hawaiian. Hanover agreed and wished he had one like it. I offered some of my shirts that I had gotten a day or so ago for him to use. Hanover wasn't the most spontaneous dresser," I explained, "so he went into my bedroom and borrowed one of the shirts. We were about the same size and build, so it wasn't hard for him to pick out one that fit.

How this is important is there were there only a couple people that didn't know I'd offered the shirt to Hanover. The murderer really fell into one of two categories: did they think it was me they were murdering, or did they think it was Hanover?"

"I see, so now you think you're the intended victim here?"

"I am certainly one of them. I think they thought it was me. If we work this thing backwards, someone tried to poison me, and then before that, someone tried to stab me in the back. You can't blame me for being a little paranoid."

"I see. And was there something that happened earlier that triggered your paranoia?"

"There is one thing I haven't told you yet." I said reluctantly.

"Just one?" she said with a hostile tone in her voice.

I proceeded to tell her about my first day at the house and how I had found the body. I even showed her the driver's license as proof.

She exclaimed incredulously. "So, you have been sitting here for the past week on the knowledge Kathleen's sister had been murdered and you didn't tell anyone?"

"I kept looking for the body to show up," I said helplessly. "But today, I realized I didn't have to keep waiting."

"Let me guess, you deduced the body was taken out in a boat and dumped into the big blue ocean."

"No. You see, Natalie had something in common with one of the guests, and she tracked it down and it caught one of them in a very interesting lie." I didn't want to say I had called her mother and under a false name, elicited information from her. Besides, I felt I was on pretty solid ground here, and when they asked around, the truth would come out.

"And what was this lie?"

"The person she talked to insisted the guest was an only child. But that was impossible," I said triumphantly.

LG put her hands on her hips. "Okay, enough with the cloak and dagger. So now you are pointing a finger at who, Kathleen?"

I wanted so much to say Rhonda again just to get her reaction, but I was walking a thin line and had marginal credibility here, so I told her who the murderer was. "It's Kathleen," I acknowledged.

LG shook her head. "Here we go again. But this time I am not following you down the rabbit hole. How do you explain her dead sister?"

"There was no dead sister. Remember, Kathleen was in theater. She made the whole thing up. She was the one in the bed with make-up on hoping to scare me away. It almost worked. But when I didn't go, that's when she decided to get rid of me. When she accidentally murdered Hanover instead of me, she decided to poison my vodka. Natalie found out the truth about her not having a sister. So, you have to ask yourself, who was that other person who came down on visits when Kathleen couldn't come? It wasn't a twin sister—it was just Kathleen in disguise. I also think Kathleen isn't going to be able to explain where she was when the other two guests, Benny and Olaf, were murdered."

"What about the letters?"

Yes, what about the letters. That was the only fly in the ointment. "I don't know if she was involved in that or not, but it doesn't really make a difference. In each case, Kathleen had the means, motive, and opportunity."

"You mean like Rhonda," she said heatedly.

I ignored the dig and pressed on. "I think you'll also find she had access to the top floor keycode. Probably Roger can confirm that. Also, she has claimed she was a victim in the Hanover murder."

"Wasn't she?"

"We only have her word of what happened."

"She had a concussion," LG said dryly.

"Which she could've done by herself. Run into a door, hit herself with a rock, anything. It would've taken suspicion away from her. I truly believe she didn't know she was killing Hanover because I think she thought she was killing me."

"How do you jump to that conclusion?"

"Based on the fact Kathleen was the only guest that didn't know Hanover was borrowing one of my shirts. Secondly, when I walked into the hospital room, she was genuinely shocked and surprised I was alive."

"Do you know what, Mr. Russell? I think you're absolutely right," she said in an ominous voice.

"I am?"

"Yes, I should arrest you," she said loudly. "The list of charges is going to be so long. It is going to take your lawyer a week to read them." She started to reach for her handcuffs when the beach crowd came through the back gate. It was Harry and Darlene and everybody else. We both stopped and looked at them.

Harry said, "Man, you two need to get a room. You sound like an old married couple having a quarrel. They can hear you up and down the beach."

Up until then, I hadn't really realized how the sound echoed in this pool area. I looked around. "Where is Kathleen?"

"Oh heck, she left a couple minutes ago to come up here. I think she heard you two arguing and was gonna try to break it up. She's not here?" asked Harry, looking around.

"No," said Darlene. "Maybe she went in the other way."

I looked underneath the pool area at the sliding glass door that led into the first-floor rooms where Kathleen was staying. The sliding glass door was half open. I thought to myself. Okay, I'm safe out here. Then I did a quick recap of what I'd said and suddenly I froze. Natalie! It only took me a split second to make the decision and I raced out to the side gate to get to the elevator to the top floor.

LG was trying to answer everybody's questions and barked at me. "Where the hell do you think you're going?"

I didn't even bother to answer as I raced into the elevator and hit the top floor keycode. When I got up to the top floor. I saw Natalie standing out on the deck leaning over the railing. I started to race toward her, yelling, "Thank goodness you are safe!"

She glanced up and started waving her arms, yelling, "No! Stop!"

That puzzled me, so I started to slow down but it was too late. I slid across the floor and out onto the deck. I reached out with one hand and grabbed the sliding glass door handle and it snapped off. The only thing it achieved was to throw me off balance. My legs shot out from underneath me as I barreled into the railing at full speed. I saw stars. I think my right arm was dislocated because it felt all numb, and a little trickle of blood ran down my face. "What the hell?" I exclaimed.

Natalie didn't make a move to come over to me. "Are you all right?" she asked in a concerned voice.

"Natalie, what happened?" I said in a dazed voice. "You're not safe up here. Kathleen might try to hurt you."

"Oh, I don't think there's any possibility of that anymore," she said forlornly.

I looked confused. "Why?"

"Well you know the project I was working on?" She reached down and lifted up a box that had the word 'FloorD' written in bold red and yellow letters across it.

I looked at her in a bewilderment. "What are you talking about?"

"It's a new product I'm trying, it's called FloorD. And you would think by that name it could be used on floors," she said accusingly. "But noooo, after I applied it out on the living room floor, I guess I just kept right on going out to the deck. I was sitting here reading the instructions again and it said specifically it was only to be used on doors and trim and not on floors because it was exceedingly slippery while wet. Well, who in their right mind names a product with the word 'floor' if you're not supposed to use it on the floor? Their slogan was 'You'll be floored after using this! I was just reading that part when the elevator opened. I stood up and there was Kathleen.

She came running towards me with a knife screaming something about I was a bitch, and why did I interfere." She paused. "She did the same thing you did and slipped on the floor but apparently she has better balance than you because she stayed upright. She slid all the way through the doors and out to the railing."

"And?" I groaned as I slowly got to my feet.

"Well, you see it's like this…" She looked over the railing again with a concerned look on her face. "Honestly, it was like she was shot out of a cannon. She hit that railing and flipped right over it. If only she was one of those short women," she lamented, shaking her head.

I looked over the railing. The two of us were looking down and everyone else was looking up at us. In the middle of the crowd was Kathleen laying on the pool deck. Groaning. If I thought I'd had a tumble sliding into the railing, try dropping down two stories onto concrete.

At the top of her lungs, LG screamed, "Mr. Russell!"

I checked my mouth to make sure the collision hadn't loosened any teeth. With my good arm I waved to indicate we would be right down.

Natalie said philosophically. "You know, CR, I really don't think I am going to be able to give this one a positive rating."

"Look on the bright side, Natalie, it can be sold as a home security product."

"Yes, but why was she after me? I didn't do anything to her."

Yeah, how was I going to explain that? "I don't suppose you were able to contact your friends at W&M to check on Kathleen?"

"Oh my gosh. I completely forgot about that."

"I was afraid you were going to say that," I said miserably.

Chapter 23

IT TOOK A COUPLE of minutes to get downstairs. First, we had to figure out how to navigate that ice rink. I tried walking across it but that didn't work. Finally, I laid on my back and pushed off with my legs against the railing and slid across the floor until I got to the edge. Natalie had a little bit better luck on her side and was able to skirt around the edge. I hobbled over to the elevator, taking inventory.

No broken bones, and it looked like I just separated my shoulder instead of dislocating it. I moved my arm around and it was extremely sore. As we passed through the kitchen, I grabbed a towel and applied to the cut over my eye.

We made it around to the pool area. LG was waiting for us, and of course she was madder than a wet hen. I could hear sirens off in the distance and approaching quickly. The rest of the guests had been moved toward the back gate and were sitting in lounge chairs. I am sure they been told not to talk to each other, so they sat there glumly and watched the proceedings.

As Natalie and I came through the gate, LG barked, "What the hell happened up there? You weren't out of my sight for two minutes and then I see Kathleen flying over the railing. And what the hell happened to you? It looks like you were in a bar fight and lost."

I started to tell her the details, but she quickly held up her hand. "Hold it. I want you over there on that side of the pool, and you Natalie, on the other side of the pool. Right now, I've got to deal with getting Kathleen to the hospital."

Before we separated, I asked LG, "Did you find the knife? Natalie said she was attacked and that Kathleen had a knife."

LG paused for a second. "Yes, I found a knife. It was clenched in her hand."

"And?"

"It was the same type of knife that was used to kill Hanover. The handle was wrapped in plastic wrap," she said grudgingly.

Just at that moment, the paramedics came rushing through the gate to attend to Kathleen. The police also arrived, and after a brief consultation with LG, they split up and started taking statements from everybody. Everybody except us, of course. The paramedics did patch up my head and offered me a sling to put my arm in. After about an hour, the pool area was empty except for LG, Natalie, and me.

LG went over to Natalie and asked for her explanation. It was at that point I realized I had told one lie too many. LG was going to figure out that Natalie had no idea Kathleen didn't have a twin sister. LG finally finished with Natalie and told her to go back to the cottage now that the top floor was going to be a crime scene. An officer escorted her out.

LG came over to me glowering. "So, you finally stuck your foot in it too far, didn't you!"

"What are you talking about?"

"Your girlfriend's account of what happened was pretty straightforward."

"It was?"

"Yes, I had one of the officers go up and check, and damn, that floor is as slippery as ice. It was actually a good thing the Nutty Professor had been testing out that floor product or she'd probably be dead right now."

"I've always said Natalie dances with the angels."

"Yes, the one thing I don't get is your story." She looked at me the same way a cat looks at a mouse.

"My story?"

"Yes, the part where you said Natalie was the one who knew Kathleen didn't have a twin sister."

"What's wrong with that story?"

"Do you mean other than the fact it is patently untrue?"

"Okay, I admit I made that part up, but the fact is Kathleen thought it was true, and that's why she acted the way she did. I really didn't intend for it to end this way. I didn't know she would overhear our conversation."

"Then how did you figure out she didn't have a twin?"

I was thinking about blaming Harry but that would just open up a whole new can of worms. I told her the simplest lie I could think of. "I guessed."

"You guessed?" she said incredulously, with raised voice and eyebrows.

"Yes, after the first day, I kept looking for the body of her twin sister and it never showed up. Then I finally realized everything would make more sense if she didn't have a sister. So if you take away the fact her sister ever existed, then you also take away the fact Kathleen was hit on the head, but rather hit herself on the head, that she didn't know Hanover had borrowed my shirt, and that she had access to the top floor, then she becomes the most natural suspect."

An officer came up to consult with LG. She moved away to talk in private with him. She nodded her head and came back.

"I'm not saying I believe a word of what you just said, but we searched Kathleen's bedroom and found a second cell phone."

"Does it have a credit card holder on the back with red and white flowers on it?"

She grudgingly admitted it might.

"That's the one I saw the first day I got here."

LG shook her head. "Even if all of this is true, what was her motive?"

I said sadly, "Her Father." I then proceeded to tell her with full orchestration and three-part harmony a mix of what Kathleen's mother and Roger had said. "She blamed all of them for her father's death."

"Okay," LG said in a tired voice. "Let's go down to the station so you can tell the whole truth for a change and we can get all this in writing."

I straightened up and tried to look confident. "Right, the whole truth, and nothing but the truth. That's me!"

"Sure, that's you all right," she said acidly.

Needless to say, I spent the night in jail—half of it explaining myself and the rest on the second most uncomfortable cot in the history of mankind. The first most uncomfortable one was in the next cell, and I had already experienced that one before.

They let me out the next morning and I took an Uber back to Goombays to pick up my car. I drove back to the cottage and breathed a heavy sigh of relief.

I came inside and sat down on the couch. Natalie came rushing out of the bedroom asking if I was okay. "It's been a long night," I said.

"Well it looks like we solved it!" Natalie said. "I knew we would. You're so wonderful."

"We? We solved it?" I eyed Natalie suspiciously. "What are you up to?"

"What are you talking about?" She said innocently. "Oh! I was just simply giving you a compliment. Why do you always act so suspicious?"

"Ah huh. I noticed your suitcase by the front door when I came in."

"Oh that, I wanted to talk to you about it. Monica and Jessica just got down to Emerald Isle. I figured I would pop down there for the next week since they also have a beach front cottage. You don't need me here anymore since I already helped you solve this, do you?" she questioned gayly.

"You helped me solve this?" I said slowly. "I am still a little unclear on that. And how exactly did you do that?"

"By being here to support you. To give you the benefit of my expert advice and support," she said enthusiastically. "You know you can't have me all to yourself. I need to spread this wealth around."

"And this wealth would be referring to what exactly?"

"Oh, my knowledge, cunning, and experience. I can't wait to tell everyone how I trapped a killer."

"Yes, I'd like to hear that story myself."

"Oh pooh, don't be a humbug. Help me get my suitcase out to the car."

I sighed heavily, got up, dragged the suitcase down the stairs and stuffed it into the trunk of the car. While it was easier going down then coming up, it still made my arm ache.

"Don't worry," Natalie said, "I'm not leaving till late this afternoon. We can still have breakfast or lunch."

"I'm too tired for breakfast. Let's do lunch. I think for now, I'm just going to go inside and work on the computer."

"Okay, that sounds like a good idea. I left my computer out so I could work on it too. I still have to figure out how to do the write up on the FloorD. I can't really call it a success but then again, I did catch a murderer with it, so maybe it's successful in its own way," she mused.

"Yes, go with that." I can't say I was surprised to see Natalie leave. I think she'd been itching for a new adventure for the last day or so. Since all the excitement was over with Kathleen in custody, I think she felt comfortable enough to leave me on my own for a while. I loved having Natalie around because she was so fun and energetic, but I think I'd had enough fun and energetic for one week. I was ready to just kick back, slow down, and relax. Maybe even do a little fishing.

I powered up my computer and puttered around on the Internet for a while until I remembered Roger had sent me a copy of the contract everyone signed for the house. I pulled it up and started reading through it. It had the standard language like 'party of the first part' and 'party of the second part' but I've read enough contracts over time where I felt there was something a little off about it. It was like some of the language was cut and pasted from various different contracts into this one. Individual pieces sounded good, but the language was different enough, so it didn't sound like it came with one voice but rather a whole chorus. I looked through it again and I really couldn't find anything dramatically wrong with it other than some of the weird conditions it had in it.

I was scrolling down through the last page, which was where all the signatures were, when Natalie wandered by. "What are you doing?"

"I'm reading this contract of Roger's."

"Oh, is Roger French?" Natalie asked, looking over my shoulder at the computer screen.

"Well that's an interesting question from out of the blue. Why would you ask that?" I asked curiously.

"At the bottom of the page in the footer," she said, pointing. "It's got all those French words, so naturally I thought it was French."

"No, I don't believe he is."

"Oh." With that she wandered over to get her computer, sat down at the table and started plugging away at her review. This was actually one I was going to read. I couldn't wait to see how she spun it.

Lunchtime came and we went to Chili Peppers Grill & Pupuseria for lunch. I was surprised the Outer Banks had a restaurant that served pupusas. Chili Peppers has been on the Outer Banks for more than twenty-five years. It was started by a guy named Jim Douglas. Jim was also the guy that coined the term 'OBX'. It was located at milepost 5.5 if you ever want to go. We were both hungry, so we decided to order an appetizer and finally settled on the Chimichurri Oysters. They were sautéed in their national-award-winning chimichurri sauce and served with house-made crostinis & shredded parmesan.

The Po' Boys sounded really tempting for lunch. They were golden fried scallops, shrimp or oysters served on toasted Cuban bread topped with southwestern cheese. But how can you go to a Pupuseria and not order pupusas ? The order came with four handmade grilled thick corn masa filled with mozzarella and a choice of bean, pork or shrimp. It was served with special sauce & slaw, beans & rice. I ordered one pork and one shrimp and Natalie got one shrimp and one bean. The sauce and slaw when added to the pupusas was absolutely terrific. We both ended up getting more slaw to eat with them. We were tempted to get the cheesecake for dessert, but neither one of us had any room.

After lunch, we got back and took a nap. It was slow and sweet and we both fell asleep in each other's arms. Natalie woke up first and resembled the Mad Hatter when he was late for the tea party in Alice in Wonderland. Wait, it was the White Rabbit, not the Mad Hatter who said that. Anyway, she kept running around exclaiming she was late, although for the life of me I couldn't figure out late for what. But she gave me a hug, whispered sweet nothings in my ear, and told me she would see me when she got back in a week, and off she went.

I went and fixed myself a V&T, grabbed a dish of honey mustard and onion pretzels pieces, which advertise to be bursting with flavor. And they were pretty darn good, I'll tell you that. I went onto the front deck to watch humanity pass by. I had just sat down when LG pulled up in her cop car.

She took her time getting out. She looked around, walked past my car and stopped to see the new windshield. She looked up at the deck, and I waved to her to come on up. I sat in the chair, sipping my V&T. "Lieutenant Gull, we've got to stop meeting like this," I exclaimed pleasantly.

"Where is your girlfriend?"

"Oh, she left," I said nonchalantly.

"I can completely understand why."

"No, not like that," I said in an exasperated tone. "She went to meet some friends down in Emerald Isle."

"I see. Well I'm sure you'll see her again when she runs low on sanity."

"Now, Lieutenant Gull, was that a kind thing to say? After all, she bagged a murderer for you."

"Oh, she did, did she?" LG stated with raised eyebrows.

I smirked. "Well that's the story she's going to tell."

"Ha, ha, have you read the OBXToday online column this morning?" she asked.

"No," I said sarcastically. "I was otherwise occupied by the guardians of the law."

"You should pull it up on your phone and read it," she said with a blank face.

I pulled out my iPad and brought up the article. It was written by Brandon. 'Kill Devil Police Crack Multi-State Murder.' The article went on to say because of detailed police and exhaustive detective work, they were able to arrest one Kathleen Kidd for the alleged murders of Benny Goodman, Olaf Raehnegin, and Hanover Bennett. It went on to say a bunch of flattering stuff about LG and her devotion to service and her attention to detail. I started to get a little nauseated. I put down the iPad. "What does this guy want to do, marry you?" I complained.

"I assume, being a reporter, he was only telling the truth," she said firmly.

"Ah huh, yeah, reporters have no hidden agendas whatsoever." I rolled my eyes and took another sip of my V&T.

"So, tell me more about this incredible deductive reasoning you went through to capture this multi-state wanted criminal," I queried.

"Well, once we got a deeper look into Kathleen's background, we were able to determine that she was an only child and had been seen in New York on a security camera on the same day Olaf died. In addition, we ran down that Kathleen had purchased rat poison three days ago at Ace Hardware. Although she paid cash, the manager there took a special note of her because she seemed to be acting 'a bit odd' as she put it. Oh, and by the way the fingerprints on the knife that was supposed to murder Natalie, they were yours."

"Sweet," I mused. "I will admit there have been times I've wanted to do that myself but..." My voice trailed off.

"It seems everywhere we turn, we're bumping into new clues," continued LG. "Once we started talking to Kathleen about what we found out, she started screaming out a confession."

"Screaming?"

"Yes, blaming everybody and their mother about what was wrong with her life and how her father had been wronged. She yelled out that you were part of the axis of evil and a key part leading to Armageddon."

I shook my head sadly. "So, it's off to the booby hatch for her?"

"No, actually that part I believe," she said with a deadpan face.

"Very funny."

"Well, either she is the greatest actress since Hedy Lamarr or that woman has lost her marbles."

I cringed at the Hedy Lamarr reference. "So where does that leave us?"

"There is no us." LG said shortly. "There's only you and me."

"I guess what I meant to say is why are you here? Are you going to arrest me again?"

She looked a little uncomfortable. "No, I guess I just came by to..." She paused.

I stood up from my chair. "My God, you're here to thank me? To apologize?"

She pursed her lips. "You're not going to make this easy on me, are you?"

"Why should I? You threw me in jail..., twice. You berated me at every turn. And all I was trying to do was help."

"You interfered in a police investigation," she said as her voice started to rise. "You withheld evidence and have been a general pain in the ass." She got ahold of her temper and took a deep breath. "Fine! I'm here to say thank you. This case closed a lot quicker because of the information you provided. Eventually." She paused and then added, "It would have closed a lot quicker if you'd been more forthright and honest to begin with, though."

I grinned. "You're not supposed to follow a thank you up with an accusation."

"Dammit, Mr. Russell." She took another deep breath. She put her face into what I am sure she thought was a smile. "When do you leave?"

"End of the week, Sunday, just like everybody else."

"Well, safe travels and do try to stay out of trouble. I'd hate to have to arrest you again." And with that, she held out her hand and I shook it. She turned and walked back to her squad car and left.

I respected her for that. It couldn't have been easy to admit I had helped her, but I knew the last part of her statement was a lie. She would love to arrest me again. I sat down on the chair and sipped my V&T. The sky was lighting up with pinks and blues as the sun slowly set over the houses. I sat watching it a while and then the phone rang. I picked it up and it was Roger.

"Hey hey. I understand we've finally got some good news."

"Yes, looks like Kathleen was the one behind everything after all."

"I had every confidence in the world you'd pull it off. I will be down there tomorrow for the meeting instead of Saturday. Figured I might as will take the bull by the horns."

"But I thought you had to stick around on the job you were working."

"No, we were able to get ahead of schedule because the owner left us alone the last couple of days. She's not back for another week, so I'm leaving a crew here to finish up."

"Great, what time are you getting in?"

"I'll be down there about midday. Anything I can pick you up at the farm stand?"

"Morris'?"

"Of course, unless you have a preference for Powell's. I could stop by there."

"Either one. But pick me up some North Carolina peanuts. You know, the kind you have to shell, lightly salted."

"Okay, will do buddy. See you then." And then he rung-off.

———Ξ———

Chapter 24

I KNEW THE NEXT morning, there was something I had to do before I left. I looked up the address and drove over there around nine o'clock in the morning. Rhonda apparently did a little bit more than catering, and it appeared she had a brisk take-out business as well. I parked and went inside. The bell over the door jingled as I entered.

Rhonda was behind the counter laughing with one of the other caterers and turned to me when she heard the bell. The smile quickly died on her face and was replaced by a frown. "What are you doing here?"

I'd had the forethought to stop by Publix on the way over and got a double bouquet of flowers. I was hoping it would soften the effect of seeing me again. Obviously, the flowers were a little overrated. "I came to apologize."

"I'm not talking to you."

"Well that's kind of silly," I exclaimed. "I mean, it wasn't like you actually murdered anybody."

That got me an even more severe frown and she crossed her arms in front of her chest. "Just the very fact you would accuse me of it was enough."

"You're right, and I was wrong. I brought you flowers." I held them out to her.

"Humph!" she said, but I could tell she was softening up just a bit.

"You heard we caught Kathleen."

"Yes, I read about it on the local news."

My arm was getting a little tired holding the flowers out, but I remained steadfast. "And accusing you of murder was a natural mistake anybody could make."

"Ha!" she exclaimed, taking a quick look at the flowers.

"I'll do anything to make it up to you."

She blew out her breath and grabbed the flowers. "Let me get these in water before they die. Stay right there, I'm not through with you, mister." She went into the back room, came out with the flowers in a vase and put them up on the counter.

"So, where's your girlfriend?"

"She left for places unknown."

"I knew you couldn't keep her," she said spitefully.

Why does everyone keep thinking that? "She went to visit her girlfriends down at Emerald Isle," I said defensively.

We stood staring at each other. Finally, she broke the ice by saying, "Okay, I'm going to take you up on your offer."

"My offer?"

"Yes, you said you would do anything to make it up to me, so I'm calling in that bet."

"I kind of meant it figuratively..." I stopped short of completing the rest of the sentence based on the look on her face. "But I absolutely meant it," I concluded hastily. "Anything I can do."

"Great, you can go and hook up with my sister."

"What?" I exclaimed with a surprised look on my face. I didn't see that coming.

"No," she said rolling her eyes and shaking her head. "Not like that. Why is it men always...? Oh, never mind. She's got a restaurant here in the Outer Banks. It's just a mile or so away."

"I don't know anything about restaurants."

"That's okay, neither did she before she got into it." She laughed. "Since you were such an expert at solving this last mystery, aside from the fact you falsely accused me, maybe you can help her out with her problem."

"I don't do mysteries. I'm an executive consultant," I said defensively. "And the rental on my cottage is up on Sunday. My home is up in Northern Virginia."

"I see," she said as her voice hardened. "So, you didn't mean what you said?"

"No, I didn't say that," I said hastily and admitted defeat. "I will stop by and see what I can find out. But again, I don't know anything about the restaurant business. I'm not sure how much help I can be."

"The problem she's having happened in the restaurant, but it's not really part of the business, if you know what I mean."

"I guess," I said skeptically. "All right, text me her address. What's her name by the way?"

"Peggy."

"What's the name of the place?"

"It's called Beulah's Biscuits."

"Beulah, where'd she get a name like that?" I asked curiously.

"It's our grandmother's name. She makes the most amazing biscuits, or she did before she died. She passed on the recipe to us, and Peggy decided to make it a go in the restaurant business."

"All they do is serve biscuits?"

"No, they've got biscuits and gravy, biscuit sandwiches, and they've got, you know, main dishes with biscuits and all kinds of stuff. It's really pretty good. She caters to two different crowds—the ones that come in for a sit-down meal and others that grab and go. Like fisherman and beachgoers. She's close enough to the beach, so she'll even deliver it right to the sand."

"Well, that's pretty clever."

"Yes, she was thinking of opening another store before these incidents happened."

"Incidents?"

"I'll let her explain that."

"If I go and see her, then we're square?" I asked hopefully.

"After you go and see her, we will be square." She said firmly. "But not before."

"Okay, it's a deal." I held out my hand and we shook hands. It reminded me of the first time we met.

I spent the rest of the morning lounging on the beach. Right around noon, I got Roger's call that he had arrived, and he asked if I could meet him at the house. I picked up my gear, dropped it off at the cottage, and then went over to the house.

"Man, CR, I am so glad you were able to figure out what was going on," Roger said with gusto. "Unfortunately, it's just created more of a mess than ever before. With Kathleen out, the morals clause in the contract, you know..." he stated confidentially, "I'm down to only four investors."

"Oh."

"Yes, Harry and Darlene, Love, Hastings and the Crump sisters."

"They didn't call you?"

"Who didn't call me?"

"The Crump sisters. They bailed and signed up with whoever is buying the shares."

"Dammit! Well, it's got to be one of those three," he said, frustrated. "One of them is buying up shares! I need you there at the meeting this afternoon or this evening."

"Why me?"

"I don't know, maybe you can be the voice of reason for these people."

"Okay, I can do that," I said nonchalantly. I tried to get Roger out of his morose mood while we scarfed down on some leftovers that were in the refrigerator. We chatted a while before everyone else started to arrive and that seemed to lift his spirits. They came in almost as a group and Roger suggested we sit around down by the pool.

Once everybody got settled, Roger started off by saying, "I know this is been a difficult year for everybody. We've lost Benny, Olaf, and Hanover. It appears Kathleen murdered them all to avenge her father who tragically died after he didn't get this house back. Had I known beforehand all the events that led up to this, I may have done something differently, but there's nothing we can do now except move forward. Things can't continue the way they are, obviously. We need more investors to offset the costs.

Hastings jumped in. "What additional costs? I don't have any additional costs. The monthly rate I pay is the same regardless of who gets killed or who gets bought out."

"Yes, but it's unfair to expect me to have to foot those bills. And besides, one of you isn't playing fair."

"Oh?" said Love. "It was your contract that we signed. And what do you mean by someone isn't playing fair?"

"I mean someone in this room sent out letters and bought the Crumpets, Penny Truman and Decker Alvarez's shares, so if I'm doing my calculations right, while each of you own eight percent, someone else is sitting on the other 26%. Which means they own a third of the property."

Harry had kept silent up to this point but now he chimed in. "So what you're saying, Roger, is if whoever has that thirty-odd percent teams up with the other two, that would give them the fifty percent needed to force you to sell this place because you won't be able to afford it in the long run. Right now, by my calculations you are paying way over fifty percent of the mortgage."

Roger was starting to sweat. "Now let's not get hasty. I know there's a way we can work this out where it is a win for everybody."

"Well I think it'll be a win for everybody if you got voted off the island and we bought you out," stated Hastings.

Roger sat there in stunned silence.

I interjected, "Has anyone read the contract?" The question startled everybody because up to that point they had forgotten I was there.

Love looked over at me, irritated. "Of course, we've read the contract. Everyone's read the contract."

"Even the small print?"

"Especially the small print," said Hastings.

"Well, that's interesting," I said and sat back in my chair.

"Now Carlton, why would that be interesting? That's just common sense. I've read that contract word for word," chided Harry.

"Oh, really? Word for word?" And then I said in French *"Ce contrat n'est bon que pour deux ans."* I think I was close in the pronunciation, but I was hoping no one would notice.

Harry gave me a puzzled look. Darlene nudged Harry. "I think that's French."

"I know, Darlene!" he said. "I'm just trying to figure out what it has to do with the conversation we're having."

"It's in the contract," I exclaimed.

"What are you talking about?"

"That phrase is in the contract." Roger had conveniently printed out and distributed to everybody a copy of the contract they all signed before the meeting. Everyone started looking through their individual copies until they came to the last page at the bottom in the footer where that's exactly what it said.

Harry said, "Well that's just some legal mumbo-jumbo. We don't have to pay any attention to that. The fact of the matter is these are all legal, valid signatures, and he has to abide by the letter of the contract."

"I agree with you," I said.

"Well then let's talk money!" said Harry rubbing his hands together.

Roger turned helplessly towards me.

"I don't think that will be necessary," I said.

"What are you talking about?" stated Harry. "Money is always necessary."

"The interesting fact here is it's kind of funny this contract was ever written up at all. You see, the attorneys that wrote it up were Michael and Blueberry Attorneys at Law."

"So what?" said Hastings.

"Well, I checked the registry and there are no attorneys at law with that name. But interestingly enough, there was a student at Falls Church High School by that name. Apparently, he was doing a bang-up business doing contract work," I said, looking at Roger, "on Craigslist."

Roger cringed.

"Hold on a minute. Hold on a minute," cried Harry. "That doesn't make it any less binding."

"Oh, that's true, but it does sort of explain how a supposed lawyer like that put all those provisions in this contract. No self-respecting lawyer would write up a contract like this. But I have to give it to Michael, because he did give an out in the contract you all signed and agreed to right below your signatures.

I don't suppose anybody's interested in the translation of that French sentence?" I said with raised eyebrows. I then quoted what Natalie had whispered in my ear as we hugged goodbye. She said it first in French and then she translated it into English. Who knew Natalie took four years of French in high school? "It says, and I quote, 'This contract is only good for two years. After that it must be renegotiated.' There was stunned silence in the room. I turned to Roger. "Roger, when were these contracts signed?"

Roger looked down at the contract. "Holy shit, three years ago."

"Looks like you boys and girls have a lot to talk about." I got up and started toward the exit as everybody started talking at once. I went through the gate, got out to my car and drove back to the cottage, smiling to myself. No bad deed goes unpunished, I said to myself. I wonder which one of them actually sent those letters. I think it's going to prove to be an expensive lesson for one of them.

Chapter 25

I WAS SITTING on the beach without a care in the world late that Friday. I was watching the waves lap closer and closer to my chair, thinking it was a great day. Then something slowly made its way into my consciousness, and I remembered I promised Rhonda I would visit her sister Peggy. I grimaced a little bit because of that, but a promise is a promise.

After another hour, I packed up my chair and umbrella and headed back to the cottage. I looked up the address Rhonda had given me, and it wasn't far away. It was located on Beach Road right at the intersection between Kill Devil Hills and Nags Head. The beach access was just across the street and it had lots of parking.

The building looked like it had seen better days, but when I walked inside, it was well-kept. It appeared they did a lot of counter business because there was a short line waiting to get their biscuits and head back over to the beach. There was also a runner that came in, grabbed some orders, and rushed out to deliver them on the beach.

I asked to see Peggy, and the gentleman who was behind the register yelled over his shoulder, "Peggy, there's someone here to see you."

Peggy came out and I could tell right away she was Rhonda's sister. She was about the same height and build. Except this version looked a little more floured. You could tell she didn't just own the place but worked in the back making the biscuits. I introduced myself and her eyes lit up. "So, you're Carlton Russell. I've heard so much about you. A lot of it flattering, and then not so flattering, but then again," she said brightly, "it turned out to be flattering again. So here you are, let me show you around. You can see we're prepping for the dinner crowd. We're open from five in the morning until noon. Then we close and open back up at five in the evening until 8:30 p.m."

"I see, so you're just getting the show on the road this evening."

"Yes, everyone's just getting here." She started to show me around. "As you could see when you walked in, we've got tables out front and all along one side. The cash register is of course out front, but behind the scenes"—she skirted the counter and indicated I should follow her into the back room—"this is where the magic happens. There are a couple of sets of double ovens along the left wall and a counter in the middle of the room to prep everything. And along the right-hand wall are a couple of standup freezers. They're actually pretty big, but we need every inch of space because we run through plenty of orders every day."

With a flourish, she pulled the handle on one of the freezers and opened it up. "As you can see..." She stopped and her eyes widened. "Oh my God!" she screamed. "There's a naked man in my freezer. Who put the naked man in my freezer?" she screamed accusingly, looking around.

I looked inside the freezer and there was indeed a naked man in there. I went in and tapped on his shoulder, but he was frozen solid. All the other workers started to crowd around. One of the women started weeping and screaming. A voice in the crowd said, "Someone call the cops."

That was my cue to get out of there. And fast. I turned to Peggy. "I think you can take it from here. I'll be at Goombays if anyone wants me." I lit out of there like my ass was on fire and pulled out of the parking lot, burning rubber. Well, as much as my 1990 Camry can burn rubber. Usually it just burns oil. I headed back down Beach Road hunched low over the steering wheel. I saw flashing lights up in the distance and turned quickly to the left up a side street to get onto the highway. I went back down toward the cottage and turned right on First Street, then left back on Beach Road. I pulled into the Goombays parking lot, got out and went inside.

This was one of those times when I definitely needed a drink. I sat at the bar and got my V&T. After a few gulps, I caught myself mumbling to myself. I didn't think I said anything out loud but apparently, I did because I heard the bourbon & branch next to me saying, "Wait, are you talking about the bird woman?"

"The bird woman?" I said, coming out of my daze.

"Yeah, Seagull. Lieutenant Candice Gull."

"Yeah, that's her," I said sourly.

"Yeah, my buddies Jack, Tim, and Mike ran into her about a year ago, and it didn't end well for them," said the B&B, shaking his head.

"Oh, why not?" I asked curiously in spite of myself.

"Well, it was a Friday night, much like tonight, and they were out fishing. You know, surf fishing. Anyway, they had a couple of beers in them, and I guess someone complained. Next thing they know, here comes Seagull marching down towards them. Well, it was unfortunate timing because Jack was taking a leak in the ocean and had his pants down to his knees.

"She yelled out, 'What the hell are you doing?'

"And he yelled back an expletive which I won't repeat, and he said he later regretted. Well, you could tell that got Seagull pretty irritated because she ran towards him and made a flying tackle. Then she cuffs him right then and there in the surf with his pants at half-mast. And that certainly spooked Mike and Tim, so they took off. You probably never met Mike, but he's a hefty ol' boy and didn't get too far before Seagull tackled him too. I guess she still had some of that football spirit in her. She used to be a field goal kicker in high school. Anyway, she zip-tied poor ol' Mike up just like a prize heifer and then she took after Tim. Tim is a wiry old man but surprisingly fast for his age. Unfortunately, he took after the fashion of the 1990s where they rode their jeans down low. He was holding onto his pants with both hands, elbows a-flying, running down the beach like all the demons of hell were after him. But she finally caught up with him. Yessiree. She knocked him to the sand and zip-tied him up as well. Just then the cavalry arrived, but the bodies were scattered over a half a mile of beach. It got to be that whenever anybody saw Seagull coming, they just packed up and left. I'll tell you what, that woman has a temper."

I nodded my head. "Yes, I've been on the receiving end of that temper. She put me in jail twice in the last week just because of my attitude."

"Yep, that sounds just like her," he said, shaking his head.

I sighed and ordered another V&T. Just as my V&T arrived, a commotion at the entrance caught everyone's attention. Red and blue lights were flashing outside, and Lieutenant Gull came bursting through the doors.

The B&B was so surprised he fell out of his stool and exclaimed. "Sweet mother of God, have mercy on me!"

"You! What the hell are you doing?" LG shouted, pointing an accusing finger at me. "Fleeing the scene of a crime, withholding evidence, and Lord knows what else. What does it take to get rid of you!" she sputtered.

"I know, I know," I said wearily, "I'm under arrest, again." I got up, gulped down my V&T, put a twenty on the counter and was escorted out.

The End

———❒———

List of Characters

——Ξ——

Flavia Torino – CEO Adar Investments (In Sumerian, Adar meant star). It is a real estate investment company. The primary focus is to buy and sell real estate, manage commercial real estate, and invest in some speculative land and home purchases.

Mo Babu – CEO Blowhard Technologies. They concern themselves mostly around wind power technology and research. They have a couple of patents and have sold distribution rights to their technology.

Zoltan Ziffer - CEO Phoenix Corporation. It is a nonprofit which helps battered spouses recover from unfortunate circumstances.

Natalie – CR's on-again and off-again girlfriend. She's a looker and twice as nutty.

Roger Bennett – Drinking buddy of CR at the BI. When he gets in over his head, it is CR that he calls.

She who shall not be named – CR's ex-wives.

Lieutenant Candice Gull – Kill Devil Hills Police Force. A hard-nosed, no-nonsense Lieutenant who is going to catch a killer regardless of who it is.

Denise O'Hara – A foxy woman who, with the help of CR, escaped being accused of murder and has a soft spot in her heart for CR.

Reynolds - Reynolds and CR go way back and CR claims that Reynolds is one of the smartest people he knows. If CR had to have a mentor, it would be him.

Officers Fenton, Thorton, Shultz, and Hanley – Four of Kill Devil Hills PD's finest, just doing their jobs to keep peace and order.

Isadora and Theodora Crump – Twin sisters who did everything together, even talking. They owned a share of the house, but did they intend to keep it?

Hanover Bennet – Ex-air traffic controller who always shot straight and said what he meant. Did someone not like what he said and decided to shoot back?

Mr. and Mrs. Harry Patterson – Harry loved to talk, and Darlene loved to correct him when he got out of line. Which happened to be most of the time.

Kathleen Kidd – Twin sister to Kaitlyn and seems to either be lucky or in the wrong places at the wrong time.

Kaitlyn Kidd – Ill-fated for a short life and missing. Did someone mistake her for her twin sister Kathleen, or did she flirt with the wrong crowd?

Penny Truman – She was a part investor in the house and got out when she saw the writing on the wall.

Decker Alvarez – He found an easy way to get out of the contract when he received a letter. He got out just in time.

Hastings Meadow – A beach bum whose parents said he needed to stay away from the house. Were they smarter than he was?

Love Tablue – A smart redhead that seems a little too good to be true, but was she?

Benny Goodman – Victim of a hit-and-run. Was the fact that he owned part of the beach house the cause or was it just a coincidence?

Olaf Raehnegin – The second victim. Did he decide that living was just not worth it anymore or did he have a little help jumping off that building?

Trouble – A German Shepherd with a caustic sense of humor.

Recipe for Beef Stroganoff

—————⌑—————

Mother's note. This was always one of Carlton's favorite meals when he was growing up. I have had this recipe for a long time, and it is still a request by Carlton when he visits.

1 lb	Round steak (¾" cubes)
¼ cup	Flour
2 tbs.	Vegetable oil
½ cup	Onion (chopped)
1 clove	Garlic (minced)
2 lbs	Mushrooms (sliced)
1 can	Condensed Golden Mushroom soup
1 tbsp	Worcestershire sauce
½ tsp	Salt
⅛ tsp	Pepper *(heck, add as much pepper as you want)*
1 cup	Sour Cream

Roll meat in flour, brown in hot oil. Remove meat, add onion, garlic, and mushrooms. Cook gently until onions are golden. Add remaining ingredients, except sour cream. Cook until thick and bubbly. Return meat and simmer about one hour or until meat is tender--stirring occasionally. Just before serving add sour cream. Pass the grated Parmesan cheese if desired. Serve with rice or noodles.

About the Author

Carton Russell has taken the privilege of introducing the author Barry Prokop. Carlton, or CR to my friends, met Barry about five years ago in the Blue Iguana Bar in Fairfax, Virginia. I pitched the idea to talk about my life. Apparently, Barry thought it was a good idea and here we are. Barry is a native east coaster in the United States who lives vicariously through the lives of people like me. We are about the same age and he likes the sounds of his voice almost as much as I do. However, many times I have seen Barry staring off in the distance and I must snap my fingers to bring him back to this reality. That is probably why it takes him so long to write down everything I tell him. That isn't a criticism, it is just that he tends to work at his own pace and in his own way. One day I will see blank pages and the next, fifty pages scribbled with notes. Go figure. It must work for him since his notes are pretty close to what I tell him. I know he wouldn't want me to be telling you this about him, but I even had to talk him into putting his name on the book and publishing it. Authors, geeez, what a temperamental lot.

Coming Soon

———☐———

Coming in the Summer 2021

The Life and Times
of
Carlton Russell
(Book 3)

by Barry Prokop

Also by Barry Prokop

———Ξ———

**The Life and Times
of
Carlton Russell
(Book 1)**

This is a book about Carlton Russell. No one has ever heard of him and probably no one ever will. But he leads an interesting and eclectic life. Sometimes detective, sometimes instigator, troubleshooter, and sometimes friend. He wanders through life not as a superhero but just as a regular person. As you get to know Carlton, you will learn he is a man of many facets, interests, and even biases. But all in all, I think you'll find him to be an all-around good guy who is trying to make his way in the world and do good.

**Available now
in print
and on Kindle at
www.amazon.com**

Printed in Great Britain
by Amazon

62214818R00167